THE ONE TRUE STORY
OF THE WORLD

THE ONE TRUE STORY
OF THE WORLD

Lynne McFall

THE ATLANTIC MONTHLY PRESS
NEW YORK

Lines from "Diving into the Wreck" from *Diving into the Wreck, Poems, 1971–1972* by Adrienne Rich, copyright © 1973 by W. W. Norton and Company, Inc. Reprinted by permission of W. W. Norton and Company, Inc.

Lines from "Asides on the Oboe" from *The Collected Poems of Wallace Stevens* by Wallace Stevens, copyright © 1955 by Alfred A. Knopf, Inc. Reprinted by permission of Alfred A. Knopf, Inc.

Lines from "The Sirens" from *Ceremony and Other Poems,* copyright © 1950 and renewed 1978 by Richard Wilbur. Reprinted by permission of Harcourt Brace Jovanovich, Inc.; first published in *The New Yorker.*

Lines from *From a Bare Hull: A Boat Building Manual,* rev. ed., W. W. Norton and Company, Inc., by Ferenc Maté. Copyright © 1983 by Ferenc Maté.

Published simultaneously in Canada
Printed in the United States of America

Library of Congress Cataloging-in-Publication Data

McFall, Lynne.
   The one true story of the world/by Lynne McFall.
   ISBN 0-87113-355-5
   I. Title
PS3563.C362705   1990   813'.54—dc20   89-18377

DESIGN BY LAURA HOUGH

The Atlantic Monthly Press
19 Union Square West
New York, NY 10003

Second printing

ACKNOWLEDGMENTS

Parts of this book were previously published in *New England Review/ Bread Loaf Quarterly, Prairie Schooner,* and *The Pushcart Prize, XIII.*

I am grateful to the following institutions for financial support: Stanford University for a Wallace Stegner Fellowship, the University of Iowa Writers Workshop for a James Michener Fellowship, the University of Texas at Austin for a summer research grant, Syracuse University for a paid leave of absence, and the National Endowment of the Arts for a literature fellowship.

I want to thank my mother, Louise McFall, and my brother, Monte McFall, for loans that enabled me to write the first draft; my sister, Sharon Benn, and my best friend, Rebecca Holsen, for their encouragement and affection; Melanie Jackson and Gary Fisketjon for believing in the book before it fully existed; and Anne Rumsey for her editorial work on it.

My greatest debt is to Brent Spencer, first reader, harshest critic, most loved.

For my son, Robert,
and my daughter, Hope

I came to explore the wreck.
The words are purposes.
The words are maps.
I came to see the damage that was done
and the treasures that prevail.
I stroke the beam of my lamp
slowly along the flank
of something more permanent
than fish or weed

the thing I came for:
the wreck and not the story of the wreck
the thing itself and not the myth.

ADRIENNE RICH
"Diving into the Wreck"

The prologues are over. It is a question, now,
Of final belief. So, say that final belief
Must be in a fiction. It is time to choose.

WALLACE STEVENS
"Asides on the Oboe"

Prologue

The One True Story of the World—that's what he called it: the story my father told me every night, from the time I was three or maybe even before, until my mother and he got divorced when I was ten, and he went off to live on a sailboat christened *Ketch-22* that took him around the world twice but never home again.

The ending of the story was always different. Sometimes the world would end in nuclear destruction—first the Moscow explosion, people wailing and gnashing their teeth, a mushroom cloud, one last kiss, then just the black on the back of your eyelids. Sometimes it would end in the laughter of the gods, one of them with a voice like Humphrey Bogart's saying, "Play it again, Sam." Once in a while my father would let me choose. "Well, what will it be tonight, Jesse? Fire or ice? A bang or a whimper?" My heart would go wild then, beating with an alien emotion: power.

After the age of six, I usually chose the ending where we went to heaven, having learned of this unlikely possibility from my first-grade classmates. I knew my father disapproved of this choice—I could tell by the way his left eyebrow would rise, distorting his face—but my desire for a happy ending was stronger than my desire to please him. "Which ones?" he would ask then. "The good or the evil? The happy or the miserable?" "Everyone," I'd say after a moment of pretended thought. "Send everyone!" This, I knew, was an even worse sin than choosing the heaven ending to begin with. "If you send everyone," he'd say, his eyebrows almost meeting at the bridge of his nose, "it's not a real ending. The story simply begins again." Sometimes I would relent then, send only the good. But I was never happy about it, and the older I got the more I insisted on having my own way, even if this meant his disapproval.

His own favorite ending was T. S. Eliot's, though I didn't know until years later that this *was* Eliot's ending; that, in the ethics of the bedtime story, my father was no saint but a fairly well-read plagiarist. He stole from Eliot, Frost, Robert Heinlein, Rachel Carson, Bertrand Russell, Borges, Barth, Wittgenstein, and others. But he was not without imagination, since I've searched in vain through the literature of world endings (not a genre exactly, so it's taken a little research) for some of his best stories.

And it was only later that I understood he had misled me about something else: the beginning. About this there wasn't a choice. I didn't hear about God's six-day feat or Adam and Eve's affair with evil until I was older than you would believe. No, that's probably not true. I heard it, no doubt, from those same classmates who gave me the idea for my favorite ending. But it didn't sink in, it was never a real possibility—as happiness was never a real possibility for Schopenhauer, or the ellipse of the earth for those who lived in the fifteenth century. Still, I should have guessed he had his prejudice. The part where intelligence emerged from inert matter, the soul from a stone, was never convincing.

My favorite of his endings—what he called poetic justice—was the one in which everyone turned into the thing they had loved most in the world. Some became paintings, houses, a blue Mercedes; others were mountains, the beach at Malibu, an elm tree; a few turned into other people, some into books or pain, and one into absolutely nothing.

I remember my excitement the first time I heard this ending, remember clapping my hands together, asking, "What am I, Daddy?

What do *I* become?" and my disappointment at his answer: "Well, that depends of course on what you love." How could his ending depend on me? It seemed a trick somehow. I kept asking him to tell me but he wouldn't. "It's your choice," he said, "but you'd better make up your mind quickly or, like our unlucky friend, you'll turn into—*poof!*—absolutely nothing." This frightened me, as if the story had become true, the fine line between fiction and reality lost. But I still couldn't decide. "You!" I finally shouted, with more relief than a child ought to know. He hugged me then, whispered, "The End," and I fell asleep happy.

It wasn't until the second time he told this ending that I thought to ask what he became. When I did he said, "A bird on a telephone wire." And the next time: "The pond in the woods after the rain." When I saw that the choice wasn't final, that I could change my mind again and again, this became my second favorite ending—sometimes, even when the choice was mine, tempting me from heaven. I was everything from ice cream to the word *sassafras.* And once when he asked me what I'd become, I said, "The whole world." I'll never forget his reaction to that. He said, "Do you know how much I love you, Jesse?" and laughed for a long time.

A strange legacy, perhaps—scepticism and wonder, pessimism and laughter, his love and his leaving—some would say perverse. I'm not sure. I give you this memory not for its intrinsic interest, though I have great affection for it, but so you'll see that I own, by an odd inheritance, some sense of the problem of perspective involved in any attempt to tell another person what happened, what it meant.

PART ONE

If the Eye Were an Animal

"To see him standing in the trillium was to see capitalism die. I didn't ask what it would cost. I wanted him."

Torrie rolls her eyes in a way that says melodrama in the morning is hard to take, goes back to buttering a blueberry muffin.

"He's a philosopher," I say.

Torrie says, "Never take a philosopher to a party. He'll ask you the point of champagne. When a man starts asking metaphysical questions, I put my tongue in his mouth. Why and why and why. After a Saturday Night Special almost any man will say, Why not?"

Torrie is a person of principle: pleasure. On summer days I admire people like that. In winter I think they are treacherous.

"Remember Phil 101?" Torrie says. "What was that fat guy's name? The one who was always slipping you notes with strange quotations on them?"

"Harold."

"Right. *Hair*-old."

"They're the only things I remember from that class. *If the eye were an animal, sight would be its soul.* Harold said it was Aristotle's best line."

"Remember the way he would climb up the fire escape and press his fat nose to our bedroom window and wail? What was that song he always sang? *I can't live, if livin' is without you-ou-ou . . .*"

Torrie and I were roommates in college, and we have kept a promise to come together every year. She knows the way I comb my hair, frowning into the mirror at the widow's peak I loathe, and the way I grind my teeth in dreams. We have fought over unmade beds, eating potato chips when someone is trying to sleep, and whether there is a moral duty to squeeze the toothpaste from the bottom up. My faults are a part of her history; I guess that makes us friends. But I don't want to talk about Harold and I say so.

"Remember that time he brought over his pet chicken and you said that you and your brother used to decapitate chickens, with an ax? I can still see the tears dripping down his fat cheeks. A pet chicken. *Jeez.*"

"I remember."

I remember the peat dust between my toes, the goosebump neck stretched taut on the oak stump, the glint of steel in the sun, the way my brother would snicker, mimic my wince, pretend to faint. I remember trying to believe it was not my hands on the handle, not my hands heaving the perfect arc, not my hands that set the body free from the mind, the old dichotomy solved with blood and silence. My father would lecture me then—me standing there barefoot, crying, watching the last jerking flight of that headless bird: "Sissygirl. No child of mine is going to be a sissygirl. Make a fist," he would say. "Like this. Now make your will just like that fist. When you've got it right, you won't cry." My father was a hard man. But when the blade's sharp edge had been wiped clean and the sun had dried the chicken blood, we would sing in the loft at the top of the barnful of ordinary animals.

I never told Harold that. I consider telling Torrie now. But I won't. She would make what is real sound like melodrama.

"Remember what he said when I told him he'd better find another window for his nose, that I needed some sleep?"

"What's with all the Harold stories? I'm trying to tell you something."

"He turned to you mournfully and said, 'Do *you* want me to find another window, Jesse?' 'She does,' I finally told him, because you were *cry*ing." Torrie says this word with disdain, then she stands up and puts both hands over her heart, makes her voice quaver and whine: " 'The way you loved me made things matter, made everything I did seem important. Now it's all ashes.' What a loser," she says, sitting back down.

"He has a wife."

"Harold?"

"No, the philosopher."

"I think I've heard this one before. It begins in some low-lit bar—the eyes across the room, the knowing smile. He slips his gold ring into the inside pocket of his rumpled tweed suit as he walks slowly across the room toward you. Debbie Boone is singing, *It can't be wrong when it feels so right.* He takes your hand. You dance. Between dancing and sex there is very little difference. You dance all night long."

"It wasn't like that," I say.

"We'll set it to music. Maybe we can sell it to Nashville."

"It wasn't like that."

"Same song, different words," she says. "It's all sex."

For the first time I'm not sure that her fake fingernails are a front. I decide to keep the story to myself. Or maybe I'll save it for Harold, who could tell the difference between tragedy and melodrama.

I imagine meeting him on some shady street in New Haven or Hartford. First I'll apologize about the chicken and the rude suggestion regarding his nose. Then, if he forgives me, I'll say, Harold, I met this extraordinary man.

Harold will nod knowingly but eyes unleering, kind.

It didn't begin in some low-lit bar, I will say. It began in a cold clean light. There is a time in late January when for a week, sometimes two, the sun shines as though April had come. Even the flowers are fooled and begin to blossom. It was one of those days, winter spring, the sky that missing shade of blue. He asked me to go for a drive. I am no nature lover so I should have suspected myself of devious dreams. I agreed.

Harold will nod gravely, a respecter of the unwise.

We put the top down on my car, drove with the wind in our hair, laughing, too fast on the winding road. Where the road curves away from the river and up, we stopped. He took my hand to help me over the steep and slippery places to where a patch the size of a child's sandbox was covered with trillium, scarlet flowers in a domain of white.

I can see it, Harold will say.

I don't know how it happened. Say it was the trillium. Or maybe it was the suncut snow on a mountain road. The hands, perhaps. Sometimes the slightest touch, partly fumbled, is better than good sex. Maybe Torrie is right—I have a talent for melodrama.

And Harold will say: Love, maybe.

It went that way for a while, then the moon made it worse. He taught me to trace the tracks of familiar stars—Sirius, Arcturus. He brought me mushrooms from the forest, fossils of intricate insects now extinct. A perfectly smooth round stone.

Ah, Harold will say, fitting reply.

And then, because he has listened in the right tone of voice, I will bring the old news: But his wife.

Harold will frown slightly, a master of tact.

His wife has been calling all week. She always says the same thing: I want you to leave my husband alone.

Not an unreasonable request. What do you tell her?

I tell her I love him.

And?

She cries.

And then?

I say I have to go. I hang up the phone, quietly. I do not hate her, no.

In counterpoint Harold too will sigh.

Then I will put to Harold the question as old as *Why the world?*: What should I do?

Harold will pause, thoughtful in his slowness, his substantial weight a gift, and say: I think you'd better find another window for your nose. So to speak.

The telephone is ringing. Torrie answers it, hands it to me.

"I want you to leave my husband alone," she whispers, hoarse from her litany of pleading. I cannot imagine her face. She is only this voice.

"I love him."

"He's married," she says. "My God, he has *three* children." As if two would not be sufficient to move me. "Think about what you're doing," she says, in my mother's distant voice. She waits. "Is he there now? I know he's there."

This is something new, and I don't know what to say. She begins to cry, and I wonder if there is causation at a distance, if my life is this one philosophical puzzle, if I am the cause of this pain.

I remember a story in the paper a long time ago, that came true in Tucson or Phoenix or Mesa, maybe Tempe. Linda, a twenty-one-year-old "coed," had been dating a married man. Her parents forbade it but she wouldn't give him up. One night, after a quarrel in which certain names would not be forgotten (slut, whore, tramp), Linda left the house and didn't come home. She lay in his arms all night long, her parents growing feverish with worry and rage, fear-lined faces against a dark window.

They wanted to teach her a lesson, to wake her up. "Wake her up" was in quotes. Linda had a dog she loved, Beauty, a German shepherd rescued from the pound. The dog was the ticket, they decided.

They drove out into the desert—the parents, Linda, and the dog. I imagine the three of them in the cab of a white pickup truck, two faces set like plaster of Paris, grim and self-righteous, Linda's eyes wandering to the desert and beyond, wondering what, the dog dozing in the bed of the truck. Say it is a day in late August, when the desert sun bakes human brains at 120 degrees. Sweat tracks their faces, eats at their nerves like acid. A hot wind blows tumbleweed across the highway empty except for these three, four counting the dog; a Joshua tree now and then the only furniture in this inhuman plane.

When they are far enough out they stop, pull off to the side of the highway. Her father takes the pistol from the glove compartment, wakes the sleeping dog. He points to the animal, hands Linda the gun. The sight of the pistol catches the light. He says, Go on.

Maybe they explain, maybe they are silent. This part is the hardest to imagine. Linda, hands inept on the gun, looks at the German shepherd; her eyes go to her parents' eyes, then back; perhaps she remembers the warmth of her lover's hands in the long night. Then the sharp sound echoing down the desert.

Linda shot herself.

I try to imagine their faces, the plaster cracking, the rush to hold her before the lovely body stops, where the gun falls. I cannot.

I find the last line of the story intact in my memory: *Police said no charges could be filed against the parents, except possibly cruelty to animals.*

The crying has stopped. She is waiting. I believe I can hear her three children breathing in the distance.

"He's not here," I say. She doesn't answer. I tell her I have to go, hang up the phone.

"The other woman?" Torrie asks. I sit staring, tracing a triangle in the crumbs on the wooden table.

She says, "What's so holy? If you can walk on water you don't need a bicycle."

"What's that supposed to mean?"

"It means you're human." I study the blood-red tips of the fingers of her left hand as she speaks.

The telephone is ringing again. Louder, it seems.

"Shall I answer it?" Torrie asks, giving me a conspiratorial grin. I let the smile die in her teeth.

She will not give up.

"Well?" Torrie asks.

My father's words rattle inside my head like chicken bones, Aristotle's best line. I wonder if there is mercy at a distance.

"Well?" Torrie repeats.

I count to fifteen, making a fist, then I reach down and slip the small plastic clip from its jack.

The ringing stops.

I can hear her three children breathing, I can feel my heart beating as we sit there looking at each other, just looking at each other. Like this.

The woman in the Mendocino Lake Lodge has been out praying for peace. "Me and some women from my church," she explains, making the beads of her rosary click, and I remember a sign over the altar of my childhood: God is Love. "I'm sorry you had to wait."

"Oh. Well. *Peace.*"

"We don't get much business this time of year. Your luggage in the car? I'll just turn up the heat while you two go get it. We keep it low to save . . ."

"No luggage," I say, looking down at my empty hands, honest knuckles.

Now it's her turn to say, "Oh. Well."

He signs a made-up name and address on the card she pushes toward him; she hands him the key to our new home.

"It's up those stairs, to the left," she says doubtfully, crooking her finger like those yellow signs on the highway that mark a curve in the road.

"Yes," I say to her unspoken question: Are you sure you want to do this? Is this what you really want? Yes.

I can hear the beads of her rosary click as we go up the stairs. Peace. Love. It's a full-time job.

The walls are turquoise and the bedspread is red brocade; from the wall sweet Jesus watches every move we make. The sheets are stamped Mendocino Lake Lodge, the two cups on the water-stained dresser are plastic, and it's sixty degrees under the covers.

"What was your name again?" I ask.

"That's not funny," he says and looks sad.

I decide to amend one of my absolute principles: Never love a married man with no sense of humor.

He takes a paper bag out of his down jacket, takes a pint bottle out of the bag, unscrews the top. "Pret-ty tacky," he says, pouring some dark rum in a plastic cup.

"Oh, I sort of like it. Some things are so bad they're good."

"Yes," he says, touching my breast.

Let us pray.

He is fond of performing thought experiments, naked.

"Suppose you woke slowly from a deep sleep. You discover a stranger's body in your bed."

"That's happened once or twi—"

"Your own."

"What?"

"Two neurosurgeons have come in the night to perform a little operation while you lay dreaming. They've taken your brain and placed it in another woman's body."

"What did they do with my body?"

"You're missing the point."

"What's the point?"

"Would it be *you*?"

"Who else?"

"Consider. You think you are remembering your first lover . . ."

"His name was Dominic Galindo. He had black black hair, the kind that goes with an eternal five o'clock shadow when the beard's gone. Eyes the color of—"

"Or was it *her* first lover?"

"Maybe both. From what I hear, the guy got around."

"Which is it? And how can you tell?"

The body remembers every extraordinary kindness.

"There are practical problems as well. Whom do you go home to? Her husband or *your* . . ."

"Consider this," I say, climbing on top of him.

Driving home from the Mendocino Lake Lodge at one in the morning. The snow makes ice sculptures of birch trees; it covers the road. I drive slowly, trying to see where the white line cuts the lane in half. A flashing red light behind us suggests I have gotten it wrong.

"May I see your license, Miss?" a man in a blue uniform says, shining a light in my bloodshot eyes.

I decide this is not the time to strike a blow for women's liberation and do as he says.

"How long have you been here?" he asks, a friendly enough question.

"Years," Aristotle says, thinking this will strengthen my case, prove my stability.

"This license is not valid in New Hampshire after two months in the state. Your registration, please?"

I rummage in the glove compartment and come up with something expired. I hold it out to him, praying he will be struck with aphasia, night blindness.

"California license, expired Texas registration, New Hampshire plates? Is this your *car*, lady?" He goes back to his car, to make a call, I suppose, and comes back with another cop who must have been hiding somewhere in the dark.

"How much have you had to drink?" the second blue man asks.

"A couple of drinks, earlier in the day," Aristotle says. Not a lie really, just an incomplete truth, such as we all make do with at times.

"Will you step out of the car, Miss?"

I look hopefully around but there is no one to save me.

He makes me do all the tricks. "Put your arms straight at your sides, put your head back, shut your eyes." Now see if you fall.

I keep my eyes open a slit and pray, an old childhood prayer. *Dear God, if there is a God, save my soul, if I have a soul.*

Arms out, a drunken scarecrow, try to touch each nose.

My brother would be proud. We used to drink ourselves blind, then practice for just such an occasion. The human arm, he would lecture, was constructed precisely for the purpose of passing drunk driving tests. Given its length (here he would demonstrate), if you extend the arm, straight out to the side, bend only from the elbow—that's very important—then you can't miss your nose, even legally dead.

The cop looks depressed. Only one more chance to keep this from being a wasted night in White River Junction. "Walk a straight line, heel to toe."

I look down at my boots, consider the height of the heels, the depth of the snow. "I couldn't do it sober," I say, realizing the implication of these words too late.

"Try anyway."

I leave an inch at least for stumbling room, hoping the dark will hide me, thankful for my big feet.

There is polite applause from inside the car, and I bow slightly.

Disappointed at my success, the cop gives me a ticket for an invalid license, no registration, and driving too slow in the fast lane.

I get back in my car, a qualified triumph, still shaking.

"You were terrific," Aristotle says, something he never said at the Mendocino Lake Lodge.

I start up the car, wipe the frost from the windshield and the rearview mirror, pull back onto the highway.

He is silent on the slow curve up the river, and I know he is thinking about his wife. Sarah. Where is she now? Asleep in their bed? Standing at a window wondering where he might be? A late cup of tea, perhaps, the steam condensing on the dark glass.

"It won't go," he says at the intersection of Wheelock and Main.

I've heard this before, at other intersections. I used to think that the fact that he kept changing his mind meant he would finally give me up for good. Then I decided it meant he couldn't. Same evidence, opposite conclusion. What does that tell you about evidence?

"This time I mean it," he says. "I'm getting too old for this. Let me go peacefully into senility." He touches my wrist, a gesture of comfort or contrition. "This time I mean it," he repeats, thereby multiplying doubt.

I shift into second and the gearshift knob comes off in my hand. The machine as symbol for ourselves. I start to cry, then stop, throw the head of the gearshift at the window on the passenger's side, watch the spider web of cracked glass form behind his surprised face.

The ringing telephone wakes me from a deep sleep, a dream of Lot's wife.

"I just screwed your lover," she says and hangs up. The voice is unmistakable.

I look at the clock. Eight A.M. I am late for work—writing obituaries for the *New England Tribune*. It's not a job anyone would covet. I know that, so I take my time getting there. The dead can wait. That's my motto.

I dress leisurely, burn an English muffin for breakfast, try unsuccessfully to start my car, fall down three times in the deep snow on the way to work, decide to give up high-heeled boots, change my life.

"You're late," Madsen says, rolling a sheaf of papers into a cylinder and popping it on the top of my desk, making the paper clips jump. I study his hands, the way the thumbs curve back toward the wrist, the square fat red-knuckled kind that could break your neck.

"I overslept." I wouldn't be sitting here now except that my lover's wife woke me up.

"I'm not paying you to sleep." His belly dances when he talks, his lips twitch, and I think of what the reporters call him behind his back: Lou Grant on PCP.

"I know that." I try to sound contrite but only make it to contempt.

"One more time," he says, bouncing a fat thumb in front of my nose, as if to erase a mistake in the air, "one more time and you write your own obit."

When he is gone I dial the telephone company. Sympathy has its limits. I tell the woman who answers about the harassing calls, the interruption of sleep. I ask for an unlisted number and get it, thinking order has been restored to the universe.

I spend the rest of the morning working hard on an eloquent obituary for the beloved wife of a Greek philosopher. By noon I am satisfied. I tear it into small pieces and stuff the pieces into the pocket of my coat as I go out to lunch. I walk down South Main past the Bull's Eye, past the P&C, and on out of town. I take a fistful of torn paper out of my pocket and scatter it like ashes over the ground. The wet snow runs the ink of the broken words together, then they drown.

As I am coming back from drinking my lunch, I run into Aristotle. He can see by my wild eyes that I am in a bad way.

"What's wrong?"

"Nothing."

"Where are you going?"

"Back to work."

"I've got an hour and a half before my three o'clock seminar . . ."

How does he do it? Me last night, his wife this morning, now me again this afternoon.

As I slip into his silver Rabbit I tell myself that what I feel is love. We go home to the Mendocino Lake Lodge, taking a suitcase this time, to show that we have arrived at the middle class of lying.

I am coming to know her better through your body. You are gentler now. I am closer to her than to you.

Sometimes he tells me what she says. This, I think, is the greater betrayal. Why? I'm not sure. I heard a story once, in a bar in Show Low, Arizona, about a man who put his wife in the novel he was writing. She woke up one morning and there was the mole behind her left knee in hardback. There were the dishes she broke in grief—methodically dropping them, the blue flowers bursting—going for $17.95. Even her moments of passion were in neat black print. "I crave it like ice cream," she said. "I want to suck your toes." He put it all in. Then he added a few words of his own: "She was uneducated and crude but the body and the face made culture obsolete. Class or ass, those are the choices, men." She left him on page ninety-three. The novel became a best-seller. I never wanted to read the book but I'd like to know how the story ends.

"Come here," he says, reaching out for me, pulling me down, down onto the rough white sheets.

I no longer have to worry about being late for work. When I come back into the *Trib* at five minutes past three, Madsen looks at my twisted clothes, my flushed face, and snorts. "I suppose you over*slept.*"

I consider the possibilities—from simple indignation to outrage, an accident on the freeway. Too tired to lie, I spend the next two hours cleaning out my desk, keeping clips of my best obituaries for some possible future employment.

I walk slowly home, trying not to think what's next. I carefully climb the winter-rotted steps and notice an old black station wagon—it looks like a low-rent hearse—parked across the street, a blond woman in the front seat, her forehead pressed against the rim of the steering wheel; three pairs of little eyes follow my footsteps up the walk.

She has gone too far. This is what I think, but there is no outrage in it. Once inside, I lock the door, pour myself a straight shot of Bacardi. It's been a hard day. By nine o'clock I am asleep.

Again I dream of Lot's wife. Always, just before I wake, she turns back toward the city. She is instantly frozen in a gesture I cannot interpret—her mouth slightly open, her hand up, something between a halt and a wave. In the dream she has blond hair and my face.

The black station wagon is still there in the morning when I go out to get the newspaper—the kids standing by the door of the car now, swaying slightly on their feet, looking ratty and malnourished, like a lineup in juvenile court. The window on the driver's side is rolled down in spite of the snow. The blond woman pushes the hair back from her face, stares straight at me, as if I were the cause of this unholy vigil, her children's cold feet.

I go back inside, pull down the shades, try to think what to do next. I could call the police. But I don't think parking a hearse across the street from your husband's lover's house is a crime. I could call Aristotle. But what would I say? It's seven A.M., do you know where your wife is? I decide to wait. I decide to wait because there is no other choice.

At eleven o'clock that night I check my last pack of cigarettes— only two left—but I am afraid to go out, a prisoner in my own house, held captive by their watchful eyes. What kind of mother would let her children freeze just to spite her husband's lover? I want to know, but there's no one to ask.

At midnight they are still there, three small shadows under the moon, the woman a smear. The falling snow makes triangles of white in the corners of the darkening glass. I don't turn on the lights.

Finally I fall asleep. Again I dream of Lot's nameless wife, the turning toward the city, the frozen gesture of warning or farewell.

In the morning the black station wagon is gone; the tracks where I perhaps only imagined it are covered with new snow.

"Sarah," I whisper, and my frozen breath rises.

I am the stranger in this strange bed.

We are not good lovers, he and I. His fingers flinch, fumble for some familiar response, begin again more slowly.

"What's wrong?"

When he is touching me, I think of her. She no longer blames me, he said. *You,* she said, were to be my lifelong friend.

"Is something the matter?"

She is the only good voice in my head.

"What is it?"

"I was thinking about Sarah," I say, and there begins a small thrill inside me: we are the subject of this love; he is only its object. It is her hand now that I touch, the desire gone, only tenderness. I kiss her wrist, place it back on his chest.

"Sarah," he says, like a confession.

"Maybe she has another lover," I say. "Maybe that's why she's taking it so well."

He looks like somebody socked him in the stomach. Clearly this is a possibility he's never considered. He considers it.

"Well?" I ask, but his eyes are closed, his breathing is calm and steady. By the way the muscle in his thigh twitches I know that he is dreaming.

He wakes me from a deep sleep, a dream of Lot's wife. "I can't do this."

"What?"

"This."

I look at the cheap clock on the Formica nightstand beside the bed. The hands cut the face in half.

"Nobody ever gave me up at six in the morning," I say. "There must be a commandment, a beatitude, *some*thing."

He doesn't smile. His eyes are no longer blue, they've gone to gray. He looks like somebody died: me.

"Okay. If you're sure this is what you want."

"I'm sure," he says, then he holds me as if this were a lie or the last time.

He drops me off in front of my apartment, but I don't go inside. I decide to take a walk to the P&C, to clear my head, to buy a few things. Except for the burned English muffin, I haven't eaten in three days. Limbs of pines, heavy with new snow, sprinkle my face as I pass but not in benediction. It's still early; there is no one on the street.

A child with tangled blond hair and blue eyes is having a tantrum on the supermarket floor, near the frozen food section. She will not get up. She will not be comforted. (The manager has tried, several times.) Where is her mother?

A woman stands with a can of Green Giant peas in one raised hand, Del Monte blue lake beans in the other. She cannot decide. She cannot move on.

The child is red faced, screaming, banging the heels of her Mary Janes against the floor with such force that she is denting the lino-leum. (The manager is frowning.)

The woman looks down at the child, glad to be distracted from this simple impossible choice. Buridan's ass in a polyester pantsuit.

The child, flailing her small legs like a haymower, now her fists, continues to scream. The woman, still undecided, considers the child. She says, "I know what you mean."

The telephone is ringing.

"I just wanted to hear your voice."

"You've heard it," I say and hang up, continue putting notebooks and paperbacks into cardboard boxes. I look at the stack of notebooks—twenty-four, one for every year since I was ten. I open one up, from the year I was eleven, December 26, 1963, and begin to read.

> If not for dreams what would we be?
> Doomed to live in reality.
> A fate to me which is worse than death,
> For there is no peace, no freedom, no rest.
> I hate to think but still I wonder
> what life would be like six feet under . . .

The telephone is ringing. I pick it up without saying hello, stare at the receiver, waiting.

He asks if we can meet later, "just to talk."

"There's an old blues song Piano Red used to sing—'You Got the

Right String but the Wrong Yo-Yo.' " I hang up, go back to reading old notebooks, try to imagine the gloomy rhyming child I must have been, dreaming of death on the day after Christmas, no mention of colored lights or presents.

The telephone is ringing. I let it ring, put the notebooks in the cardboard box along with my favorite books—*The Shadow Knows, Sleepless Nights, Endless Love,* tape it shut.

I look at the collection of objects on my dresser: a sapphire ring with an expandable gold band, withered mushrooms, fossils of intricate insects now extinct, a perfectly smooth round stone. We must choose again and again—what to take, what to leave.

When everything is in the trunk of the car, the floor scrubbed to a shine I can see myself in, I call the landlady to say she can keep the deposit and the furniture, pin the key to the mailbox, stick the dirty rag mop and the empty blue bottle of Johnson's floor wax in the garbage can, get into the car, gun the engine, gripping the stripped threads of the headless gearshift until my hand grieves.

I stop for gas in White River Junction. A car needs gas. I decide to call back, just to say good-bye. I let it ring fifteen times but he doesn't answer.

I spend the day in the Hotel Coolidge, drinking Cuba libres. An old man plays "Autumn Leaves" on the untuned piano, over and over, leaning into the keyboard, swooning. It's winter, I want to tell him, but maybe winter is a season he can no longer imagine.

I call again, from the phone booth outside the hotel. It's getting late. I see no point in this except pain. I let it ring.

Inside, more "Autumn Leaves." There is only the old man, the bartender, and me.

"Doesn't he know any other song?" I ask the bartender.

"He owns the place."

"Oh. Well."

I have another Cuba libre, try to think of what I will say when he answers. Did Lot's wife look back from weakness or strength? From guilt or too much love? Maybe she had a lover in Sodom or Gomorrah, maybe both. Maybe she just couldn't go. Was it passion or a fascination with pain? By 11:45 I am drunk enough to say that

I am sick to death of "Autumn Leaves," but the owner of the piano doesn't hear me.

I put on my coat and my scarf, go back outside. I dial his number again, drawing lines with my fingers on the frosted glass.

The telephone is ringing, ringing. It sounds shrill in the quiet night, an insistent voice, the same question over and over. By the time he answers, it has been ringing so long that I've forgotten the point of the machine and stare at it, amazed.

"Who is this?" he asks.

"Me. Jesse."

"Where are you calling from?"

"White River Junction. The Hotel Coolidge."

"Don't go. I'll be there in fifteen minutes. Fifteen minutes," he says.

"What about—"

Click.

"Sarah," I say, and a circle of mist forms on the glass, disappears.

I walk out under the mean moon, take off my coat, my scarf, stand still in the midnight cold, wanting the world to freeze my body to fit my soul. Empty hands at my sides, I put my head back, shut my eyes tight. I imagine his headlights marking the slow curve down the river, the angle of his head, bent slightly forward, shoulders tense, his hands gripping the wheel, Bach on the tape deck, an illusion of order. I put my index finger to my nose. Left. Right. I am having to do this not with two cops for witnesses but here alone. I suppose he is at the intersection by now—Does he hesitate? Does he even think of her?—he will be here soon. I know what to do next but I cannot see the white line. I start off easy, slow in the cold night. Then I run.

What's left to call you when the popular music stops and you're humming in the dark with a split lip? I was heading south on 91 when the eight-track tape ate itself—it sounded like somebody was strangling Linda Ronstadt   then the lights went out on Interstate 90, just past Woronoco. When I slammed on the brakes I was kissing the steering wheel.

I decided to continue, not on uniformly good grounds. Traveling through the dark made me feel nearly happy: my terror had a plausible object. And I could cry then, with no self-parody, legitimately dreaming myself dead. I was a tortured child—a congenital malcontent, my mother said—but I lost my talent for suffering the year I turned ten and, since then, have not been able to cry without a script of some sort, an odd trait I do not know the source of. Perhaps it's because there is no concept of sympathy suitable for the self; there is only stoicism and self-pity.

Driving blind reminded me of playing chicken in high school, a contest I never lost because, as my brother said repeatedly, "There's a difference between courage and stupidity and you never learned what it is."

When you're playing chicken with a car, you've got to pick your opponent with some care or you're liable to end up with two dead heroes, one of them yourself. It is unwise at least to play chicken with one's equal, for the simple reason that death is not an event in the game, it's the end of the game, as Wittgenstein, who by all accounts did not play chicken, says.

I remember that winter when the boys in the band (what their female counterparts sneeringly called the jocks) thought they had found someone who could teach me the meaning of humility. He was a new man in town, Dom Galindo—tall, dark, and dangerous—straight from North Beach, San Francisco, where the motorcycle gang he managed had been dispersed—into single cells, it was said—for carving up some snotty cheerleader. Bigtime bad, compared to where we raised hell, a small town with churches on every corner and cops who stopped you out of boredom.

"You're dead, bitch," Dom said to me in the hall, thereby reinforcing this impression.

The rendezvous was set for ten o'clock that December night: Jack Tone Road, deserted and wide. I had to borrow my best friend's car—a little red T-bird—since the one I usually drove, a gold GTO, had recently been wrecked. I was afraid my affection for the car's owner would give Dom the edge, but then she pointed out that at the worst I'd be dead, and what self-respecting parent could complain about a totaled car under those circumstances? This cheered me up.

"You'll be nothing but a whimper in a dark place," Inger Sharp said to Dom at quarter to ten, and the varsity cheerleading squad cheered. "She's going to eat you alive."

"I could go for that—after it's over, maybe," Dom said, and seven big dumbs laughed.

I remained silent and dignified.

We positioned ourselves a mile apart. The cheerleaders and the jocks stood at the halfway mark on opposite sides of the road. Waiting there alone in the dark for the signal, I had a subversive thought: I could back this car all the way to Stockton. But then I remembered who I was. Jesse Walker. Ballbreaker. Bitch. I narrowed my eyes and said that name like a mantra. By the time Joey Frazier waved his ratty white T-shirt, my bottom lip was bloody, and I put my foot to the floor.

A mile is not a long distance and Dom was doing his part to make it shorter—three hundred yards away and still coming fast. The car began to shimmy, then to buck. *Two hundred.* There was the smell of gasoline, a great trembling of metal, and I imagined myself exploding, parts of my body found the next morning scattered all over San Joaquin Valley. *One hundred.* I wore dark glasses to fight the glare of the headlights but when Dom was fifty yards from defeat I shut my eyes tight so I wouldn't be tempted to swerve. The principle of the firing squad. Courage has its allies.

When I heard the cheerleaders screaming—"Give me a *D, D!* Give me an *O, O!* Give me an *M*"—I knew I'd won. "What does it spell? Chic-*ken*!" I backed up slowly—casually, one might say and surveyed Dom's yellow Chevy in the shallow water of the irrigation ditch beside the road. But where there should have been joy came an alien emotion. I decided not to stay for the crucifixion or the applause, gunned the engine, and was gone. (For this the owner of the T-bird did not forgive me.) And I never called him Chicken Galindo, even after it was shortened to Chickie and the name lost most of its history, then to Chick, only a name, no meaning.

Dominic Galindo, it seems, was a victim of his reputation, as I might well have been of mine. The motorcycle gang was a myth—their bikes were Schwinns—and the cheerleader they were supposed to have carved up was his girlfriend, killed in an automobile accident. He had a thing about cheerleaders, I later learned, and I did my best to let this fantasy live. From sympathy or enlightened self-interest, I'm still not sure. The human heart is a sneaky thing.

This is what I thought, on that cold December night—how the view changes, the voice alters—on that imagined road, traveling through the dark.

In a Dark Time

"We are considering no trivial question," I say to the mechanic at the All-Night Exxon when he quotes me fifty dollars for the inch-square piece of black plastic necessary to fix the light switch on my car. A map on the wall of the garage has an X left of Albany with a sticker that reads YOU ARE HERE.

"Nobody's twistin' your arm, lady. You want the part, you pay the price." A string of spit talks when he talks. His thumbs hang like guns from empty belt loops.

"How much could it cost, do you think, to create this little piece of black plastic. A dollar? Two? How much did it cost you?"

Grease-covered silence. He stares up into the guts of an old blue Malibu. "Fifty dollars," he repeats. "Take it or leave it."

"But why do you think it's *all right* to charge fifty dollars for what cost you five?" Spoken in the philosophical voice of an insolent child, shrill and rising.

"I *can,*" he says, and his black fuck-you eyes back him up.

I look down at the rusted license plate like a cue card on the front bumper of my car. LIVE FREE OR DIE.

Our eyes lock in an embrace.

I do a little dance, a step my father taught me as a girl—the Teaberry Shuffle, I believe he called it—get in, slam the door, gun the engine, pop the clutch, leaving rubber like a gift.

We are considering no trivial question but how a person should live.

It began to snow and I turned the windshield wipers on. There was no one on the road and it gave me the sense of being caught in one of those paperweight worlds I had wanted as a child: green plastic pines in a heavy glass ball you could pick up and shake to make it snow. I could turn off the wipers, I thought, and watch the snow slowly cover up the glass, let the world decide what would become of me. Chicken for one. But just then a truck came barreling down the mountain behind me, horn blasting, the back fishtailing as it passed, brake lights like fireflies in the darkness. My hands began to shake, then my whole body trembled—as if, even though I was too stupid to be scared, my body knew—and the trembling made me afraid. But what was the alternative? Stopping by the side of a road, the curve and edge of which are obscured by the dark, is no safer than to just keep going, so I did.

Driving in the mountains without headlights may take courage. This is the thought I practiced in the black night. I could see a car coming from behind, but I had no way to signal the driver except with my brake lights, which is not the ideal solution, especially on a down-hill grade. The driver slammed on his brakes, swerved left to miss me, then laid on his horn for miles and miles, too angry to speak or even be grateful for his life.

There were no cars or trucks for several minutes, and without lights ahead or behind it seemed suddenly quiet and I felt more alone. I fumbled with the light switch, flipping it back and forth, back and forth, as if great desire might create its own fulfillment. The clicking reminded me of crickets I had listened to at night in the house where I grew up.

As a child I thought that when I closed my eyes the world disappeared, and I would try to stay awake all night, but the heavy desire for sleep would overtake me and I would fall asleep dreaming of lost continents, tragic failures of the self.

I reached up and fiddled with the plastic switch by the circle of glass on the overhead light, which came on, blinding me, making it harder than ever to see outside—which way the road went, which way was forward, which way dead. I flipped it off and tried to adjust my eyes once more to the dark, blinking hard, opening them wide.

Another truck rumbled by and threw on its brights, as if I might not realize my lights were out. The truck was going so fast that the wind it created sucked my car into it as it passed, then threw it back, and I had to grip the wheel hard not to be flung, like a skater at the tail end of crack the whip, over the edge.

I flipped my flashers to tell the driver what I thought of him, and they came on, lit up the road ahead, the way lightning startles the sky, then the world went black again. I laughed out loud, surprised into happiness. Every three seconds or so was like that: the lights came on, then went out, came back on—and for that split second I could see the road curving right or left, a framed shot of a mountain scene at night—to the left a frozen waterfall on black slate, the drifting snow shot through with light, making the night eerie, magic. Snapshots of a dark vacation.

The next shot was of a car coming toward me, the driver's surprised face, mirroring my own, to see a car suddenly appear in the night where nothing had been. But I kept to my side of the road and it passed safely by.

The fluttering excitement in my stomach settled down and it

became clear, after a while, that my death was not imminent. I took a deep breath, pushed in a Judy Collins tape—*Midnight, not a sound from the pavement, has the moon lost her memory, is she smiling alone*— gave myself up to it, the melancholy voice, the uncertain road. Somewhere near Syracuse I began to be afraid I was immortal.

The room was so white. White ceiling, white walls, white sheets. I put my hand to my head, touched the bandage, felt the tug of the needle dripping blood into my veins or taking it out. I looked across at the other bed. A woman in a white gown, long dark hair, bandaged wrists above the edge of the sheet, palms up, waiting for something to be given or contemplating the loss.

Without looking at me she began to speak, as in a hallucination or a dream. "My life is quiet now, well-ordered, and filled with light. What my mother would call a good life. It wasn't always like this, and sometimes when I hear a harmonica played in a certain key or sudden reckless laughter, I'm forced to recall a time I would say I regret." She makes her lips tight, a thin line, as if to show disapproval of herself. "I'm a sensible woman, not prone to extravagant emotions, the mess most people call a life. But in those I've loved most, there's a streak of perversity that bears no relation to malice, a deep respect for the unwise impulse, a belief in their own necessities. Mostly they come to grief, but in this soft, shutdown day, their grief seems to me more sacred than anyone's happiness.

"Morris Brink had all three. He wasn't a rebel because rebels know what they're against. He was himself alone, a beating head without a wall, less a man than a force, which is why I never told anyone when I married him. I knew he could not be kept.

"When we met he was planning his next assault on the possible world. I'm writing a book, he said, that will destroy all the books in print. *The Seven Deadly Virtues* it was to be called. I asked him what they were and he said idle curiosity wasn't one of them.

"He could steal a tape deck from a locked car in seventeen seconds. I don't know what significance this has, but it's the outstanding fact by which my friends remember him.

"I have my own memories. The first time we made love I sobbed and couldn't stop trembling for hours—as if someone had plugged a human body into a light socket and flipped the switch. Cartoon passion. I'm a woman most people would call tough. Wary, not easily touched. But the fierceness with which he held me—I thought my bones would crack, could feel his teeth pressed hard against my teeth—ripped something essential from me, something I would not willingly give because I hold self-possession too highly.

"People will smile and say love like that can't last. Better gentle everyday affection, something steady and real. But they're wrong, it can. For a year and a half when he touched my breast my heart stopped under his hand. I'm a tall large-boned woman, not given to such displays, but he'd pick me up, whirl me around, hold me close. My pulse beat in my stomach and I'd forget to breathe. Honey, he'd whisper, and I wondered what I did before I touched him, what electricity I ran on, how lonely my skin must've been. Seven years later, I saw him—in the San Francisco Airport when I went home for my father's funeral. I cried out at the sudden assault of terror and joy, my hands ached for days, the minister's words lost, my father's last face.

"My God, the stories we tell.

"Twice he beat me, not out of anger—though I have a mouth to make a meek man murder—but from some terrible need to work his will on the world. That's what I believe. I know the words that women of a certain sort will say, how their tongues will cluck and a warrant will be sworn out for the bad name I've given my race. *People think they know what happiness is when they are really sick.* I have said such things myself. He beat me and still I stayed . . ."

"Why?"

"I am no masochist, no weak and whimpering woman afraid of the dark. For years I led a solitary life, made my way in a world of conventionally acceptable sadists—the ones who try to put you in the place they think you fit, who smile and smile and then trip you. I have eyes of my own and I've said, repeatedly, I know who you are and I saw what you did. I do not concede. You are right to ask: Why then?

"Except for the violence he was the most deeply gentle man I have known. It sounds a paradox or a lie. A black eye is not a caress, I admit."

She waits.

"It's not that I couldn't help myself, I could. I chose not to. Because the world would stop dead if . . . Some things can't be explained to the deaf."

She takes a sip of water from the sweating glass, places it back on the bedside table.

"When he walked out the door I was relieved. You can't live with your heart in your mouth that long and survive. What I know wouldn't fill a shot glass but I know that."

She looks down at her swaddled wrists. "Another time, another place. Another person.

"My husband is a good man—decent, kind, dear to me. I'm not an easy woman to put up with. There's a talent for daily living and I do not have it. I get stomachaches and bad dreams if there are not long slow days with no one in the room. I don't know if others are like this, what missing piece made me unfit to live with. But with him the fault is less noticeable. Sometimes he goes off for days, a traveling husband, leaving me alone in the empty house, the bed a place I stretch instead of hunch in, the books my own. I can breathe then, careless. And when he comes home, he doesn't hate me for it. I am grateful. No, grateful is not harsh enough. I'm amazed. Kürnberger says that whatever a man knows, whatever is not mere rumbling and roaring that he has heard, can be said in three words. *I love him.*"

She breathes with the effort of thought. The room is so white the overhead bulb seems a joke.

"But today the boy next door, a beautiful and wayward child of sixteen, was playing his harmonica out back at that stopped hour between twilight and dark, and something carefully assembled came undone. I bit the knuckles of my fist, bit hard, but still I grieved—and later wondered whether I and every lesser thing is just this: a story we tell ourselves to make it from hell to breakfast."

"The last thing I remember is when I looked up a Mack truck was coming at me."

"Life is just one whiplash after another," she says, assaulting the pillow while I lean slightly forward in the bed. Her face is cracked into perpetual sorrow above the plastic nametag. Alice Jean. "Three days," Alice Jean says. "You were out for *three days.* We were beginning to worry." She gives the pillow a last punch, then soothes it. "There now. Better?" She surveys the room, looks pleased with herself, then walks out, her white shoes squishing like waterlogged boots.

Is there anyone who has not awakened some midnight, smooth with sweat, not from dreaming but from the absence of dreams, and seen the world from outside, as if from a great height, as one not human might see, not a person but an eye, devoid of memory, desire—and, looking down from that height, beheld the arbitrary order beneath, as if a child had connected random dots—star, hand, tree—and made a picture of nothing? Even the body in the bed, known to be one's own in one's sleeping life, seems ludicrous, small, with its ratlike round of habits and hates, loves and losses, the work it does to keep itself, of trivial importance, like a pig farmer who grows the corn to fatten the pigs to buy more land to grow more corn . . . And every human endeavor—history, science, art—is the body in the bed, the child, the pig farmer blown large. Sleep is not possible in such a state, until the dawn gives back the color and substance of ordinary objects, remakes the bed in its human form of comfort, warmth, dismisses the midnight beliefs as phantoms.

After three days in the dark, the waking is like that of the dreamless sleeper, only the dawn gives nothing back.

"How do I look?" the woman in the bed beside me asks, pulling the sleeves of a yellow cardigan down over her tender wrists. She shifts her gaze from the bandages to the small compact mirror, squints.

Her name is Rebecca and she is going home today to her husband. She has combed her hair and put on lipstick, a pale shade of pink. Against the crisp white sheets her life looks possible.

"Lovely," I tell her.

With the proper shift and squint, I could go back to what memory makes of a life—consider the usual codes of human conduct a reasonable request; the common beliefs, well founded; the lover loved and left for uncommon virtues, uncommon faults. Ordinary doubts.

"Not bad for an old woman," she says and laughs, taking a last look in the compact mirror, snapping it shut.

Picture this: a woman in a hospital gown, bare ass to the wind, tangle-haired, barefoot, thumb out, at the edge of Interstate 90 at four A.M.

Within the last five minutes two cars have come so close that the hem of her hospital gown whips her legs but they do not stop. She thinks of a story she heard at the Red Dog Saloon in Juneau, Alaska. A man lost his brakes doing sixty on the only road to town from Auke Bay. The car rolled over twice, caught fire, then fell into the water. The man was thrown free. Though his shoulder was dislocated and a leg or two broken, he counted his blessings. Make that singular. Sometime later, a pickup truck driven by a drunk teenager was coming back from town. The driver didn't see the lucky man and ran him over.

An eighteen-wheeler whips by, making a parachute of the hospital gown as her fingers and toes start to go numb. She hears, as from a distance, sudden laughter, wild and deep. This is what she thinks: Star. Tree. Hand.

"Get in," the man says, then he reaches across my lap to pull the door of the pickup truck shut, locks it. "What's a nice girl like you doing standing by the side of the road in the dead of winter in nothing but a—what? Slip?"

I shiver in pleasure at the sudden warmth of the truck.

"Old man throw you out?" he asks, pulling back onto the highway.

He waits for me to answer. "The strong silent type," he says. "I like that in a woman."

I smile then but only slightly.

"Lucky Redbord," he says, putting his hand out.

I take it. Rough, gentle, warm.

"Is that a nickname?" I ask.

"No ma'am. My mother really named me that." He takes his wallet out of his back pocket, causing the truck to swerve a little, opens it with one hand, lifts a cracked yellow piece of paper out.

"Certificate of Live Birth," I read. "Lucky Redbord. Born: September 23, 1952. Havre, Montana. Mother: Lucille Ellen Redbord. Father: Unknown."

"My father was a song my mother sang just once," he says, folding the ratty piece of paper and putting it back into his wallet. "She wanted an abortion but the local butcher was the only person in that one-bar town she could get to even consider it, and he expected more than money for payment. To him, women were just so much meat."

I study his face in the pale green light of the instrument panel to see if this is a joke. Dark eyebrows drawn into a silent discourse on human folly, firm and forgiving mouth. No ma'am.

"She told me this in first grade—when I found out that most kids had a father, which I guess I knew, but did not take to be an absolute necessity before anyone brought it up. Little bastard, they said. Then I did. So I asked her about it and she told me."

I try to imagine him that little and helpless but can't. Six foot two, maybe; black boots, Levi's, Pendleton shirt; the hands of a man who has had his way, without asking.

"Told me it was a simple point of integrity, both in the matter of the butcher and of my father. Said she'd never slept with a man she didn't want and wouldn't marry a man she didn't love. On account of this strict adherence to a life of principle, I had no live-in father but also was not aborted. She named me Lucky, she said, because I *was* lucky. Lucky to be alive.

"Nice laugh," he says, nodding his head slowly, as if adding something up. "Well, the next year my mother left me in Waxahachie, Texas, with an aunt and uncle I'd never met—pinched lips, dead eyes, you know the type, *du*-tiful—and went off in search of the true love she thought she deserved but had not found yet."

"Did she find it?"

"No. She's on husband number four now, I think. Some phony cowboy she picked up in a saloon in Jackson Hole, Wyoming. You know the type—big hat, no cows."

"I know. I met him in Tucson, Tucumcari, Corpus Christi . . ."

He laughs. "Where now?"

"I don't know."

"Well, there's one good thing about that."

"What's that?"

"You can afford to take your time getting there." He reaches across the seat, touches my knee.

I think of a woman I saw on the news in the late sixties—tangled black hair to her waist, a slash of sunburn beneath blue eyes, sandals, halter top, cut-off Levi's—being interviewed by a three-piece suit with a microphone attached to the necktie at an on-ramp of the Santa Monica Freeway. "Why," he asked, "do you continue, knowing the danger?" In the previous week there had been three rape-killings of hitchhikers, the high school pictures of three girls in Peter Pan collars and the same face flashed over and over on the screen. She said, "I do it cuz I dig it." It seemed a good enough reason then. Now I wonder. Was it the danger she craved or the peace that followed it? Or the hope of a better place?

"Where am I?" I ask, trying to get my eyes to focus, pulling the hem of the hospital gown down over my knees, feeling the cold Naugahyde seat cover beneath. Who is this? How did I get here?

"Howard Johnson's. It could be anywhere."

"I feel like a rat slept in my mouth."

"Here. This might help." He hands me a white Styrofoam cup of coffee.

"Thanks." I take a sip, shiver, feel the hairs rise on my arms.

"You might find something to put on in that duffel bag behind the seat. It won't be satin but it'll keep you from freezing your ass off."

I hand him the coffee, get the bag out, choose a gray flannel shirt, faded Levi's, black socks, put them on while he watches. What is propriety to the freezing?

"Matches your eyes," he says, giving me the coffee. His hand trembles and I take back something I'd thought.

"The shirt or the socks?"

He doesn't smile, starts up the truck, turns on the heater, wipes off the rearview mirror with the back of his wrist. I want to touch his large graceful hand but I don't dare. Strangers do not touch each other except in strange beds, and then only for sexual purposes.

"Maybe it's none of my business," he says carefully, "but did your old man do that?"

"No. I lost the right of way to a Mack truck."

He doesn't talk then for a long time. I want to ask him a question but he is no one that I know.

I watch the mileposts and the green rectangular signs as if they carried a clue. Nothing else to look at but infinite expanses of snow and shadow, an exit now and then—to Elyria, South Bend, Chicago.

"Dubuque, 27 miles," he reads. "We're almost home."

Home.

I imagine that this is my father, Alex Walker, at thirty-four, the same age I turned today. That was the year he gave up stock-car racing for a desk job at Massey-Ferguson, a job he hated, a job he brought me home green duck-billed caps from but no trophies. I am the little girl in the white dress, age nine, clicking the heels of her black patent leather shoes together, happy to be in the front seat of the silver-blue hardtop with him instead of in the old black Packard with my mother, sister, and brother, miles behind. It is night. We are driving back from San Jose, doing eighty through the Santa Cruz Mountains, straightening the curves out, as he calls it. I am not afraid. I have one hand out the window, making figure eights in the wind. He is drinking J&B out of a silver flask—it flashes in the lights of the oncoming cars—happy because of the trophy on the floor between our feet.

He tells me again. "The secret to winning is in not lifting. You have to be able to keep your foot to the floor when your car is in flames and the wall is coming at you." He reaches out and puts his arm around my shoulder, pulls me in, rubs the stubble of his day-old beard against my cheek. "Lifting is to winning as choking on a chicken bone is to breathing . . ." I say it for him: "Fatal." He smiles as if I were the cleverest child in the world.

I look at him, squint, but the likeness won't hold. Still, maybe he would know. Did the father walk out on his life because he was tired of telling the story? If not, why did he go? And what was the lucky man's last thought before the wheels of the drunk pickup truck

ran it down? Can you feel deep grief for an instant? Or was it this—
free! Did the woman on the six o'clock news ever find out why anyone
did what she did?

Across the dark cab he smiles. "Almost home," he says again.

Should one say that, even at the last, Alex Walker didn't lift?

Star, Tree, Hand

Suppose you wake slowly from a deep sleep. By the clock it is midnight. A quarter moon cuts your thigh, misses your face. Where are you? What? Only this slow waking, no clue to who you've forgotten you are except the snow on the sill of the window, your own eyes.

This bed you don't recognize—white sheets turned back to a deep blue comforter—or the way the shadows play what must be trees along one wall. Your room, you guess, like some psychotic detective investigating the mystery of her own disappearance. But how can you tell? There is no evidence of struggle, no stranger by your side, only your strange self. Who are you? What is the nature of your crime?

Perhaps you are a waitress, late for the midnight shift. Even now, your fellow workers frown and wonder where you are. (Is it like you to be late?) The customers, impatient, stare at the door, their plates of pancakes and scrambled eggs growing cold beneath the heat lamps.

No. It's too unlikely.

How do you know? There are some general truths you remember, imagine still hold—that snow suggests a winter and guilt implies a crime. But general truths are useless in this case. Syllogisms will not save you.

You try to place yourself in time. What midnight is it? Winter, but what month? The moon isn't talking. A calendar would help, but you'd have to know where to look in the dark room. And even so, the calendar wouldn't tell which month it is, only a page; a number for each day but not the day.

The mirror! Perhaps the mirror will give you back your life.

Who are you? What do you want? you ask, as if a stranger at your own door. Without the memory of pleasure and pain, you don't know. Not a bad face—the gray eyes with their dark corneas of grief, the lines that sketch a history of scepticism, arrogant bones in hollow cheeks—but whose? Somehow the crack that makes a spider web in a corner of the bright glass seems more familiar. You smile. You smile to see what it looks like but there's nobody in it. An animal's consciousness, fear and no history. It smiles and hands you back your eyes, empty.

Perhaps you should hire a detective—the famous sleuth, what was his name? Ha! You don't even remember your own. How can you look up a word in the dictionary when you don't know how to spell it? A childish question of high seriousness, you see that now.

Maybe the man who fits the clothes in the closet has gone out for ice cream. How sweet! (Which flavor do you like—chocolate? Vanilla? Pralines 'n' cream?) At any moment he'll come home, through some door you cannot yet imagine, and tell you your name. What do you think? What are the chances of it?

Small. Nearly none. You who scorn weakness whimper quietly beneath the cool sheets.

What do you do now? You decide to wait. You decide to wait because there is no other choice. (How clever you must have been when you were . . . someone.)

Then it comes to you—the thought that assembles the dark: When there is no story one can tell, no story at all, here there is certainty.

Deserted by everything that matters, you sleep.

I wake to the smell of bacon frying, see the hospital gown on the arm of the bentwood rocker, the borrowed clothes on the floor beside it. Then I remember the accident, the hospital, the knight in the white pickup truck.

I get up, dress quickly, an old habit from home: my father would promise each of us kids a dollar if we could get dressed in under sixty seconds.

He is standing at the stove, cooking eggs.

"Ah have always depended on the kindness of strangers," I say in my best Blanche DuBois.

"You're up early," he says, not looking at me.

"What about you?"

"I always get up early. It's the best time of the day. When it's quiet . . . and there are shadows still on the edges of things."

"What do you do out here all alone?"

"Grow a little corn. Raise a few pigs."

"A *pig* farmer," I say, snuffling behind my hand.

"If I'd known you felt that way, I'd've left you on the road."

"I never met a pig farmer is all. I thought it was something people did in economics texts."

"City girl."

"No. My father killed chickens and cows."

"What does he do now?"

I snap my fingers. "He got killed in an automobile accident. Some crazy fool going the wrong way down a one-way street. Him." I shake my head.

"Sounds like a story to me."

I consider the possibilities—from simple indignation to outrage, grief. "Actually he sailed off into the sunset when I was ten. No note. Nothing."

He looks at me sceptically but lets it pass. "You ready to eat?" he asks, putting the plate in front of me. Bacon, eggs, toasted English muffin. Coffee.

"I never eat breakfast."

"Well then, I hope you don't mind watching me." He gets himself a cup of coffee, moves the plate to the other side of the table, sits down.

I watch for a few minutes in silence. The loveliest hands: strong clean angles, prominent veins, violent grace in the fingers.

"How can you stand eating that stuff after looking them in the eyes every day?"

"Pigs are smart," he says, picking up another piece of bacon, studying it, taking a bite. "But they have no loyalty." He doesn't talk then, just eats—slowly, thoughtfully, as if eating were something sacred. You can tell a lot about a man by the way he eats.

When he's finished, he gets up, takes his plate over to the sink, washes the dish and the pan, dries them, puts them away, slowly, methodically, a lover of order and precision.

"You'd make somebody a good wife," I say. "Ever been married?"

"Once. You?"

"He left me with the dirty dishes."

"Spoken like a bitter woman."

"No. After the divorce I broke them. A sort of ceremony of my own. I took every plate out of the cupboard. The dinner plates in one stack, the platters in another. Then I got the kitchen stool, climbed up on it, lifted the plates high above my head. *Crash!* Then came the glasses, assorted cups and saucers. I set them carefully on the old oak table, then, with the length of one arm, swept them against the wall." I demonstrate, moving my arm over the table, then flinging it at the wall. "Louder this time. *CRASH!*"

"What then?"

"Paper plates."

He laughs. "More coffee?"

"Yes, please."

He brings the pot over to the table, pours the coffee with a neat flourish of the wrist, as if attention to small gestures could save us.

"You haven't told me your name."

"Jesse." I put my hand out; he takes it, holds it a moment too long. Any minute, I think, he will ask for his clothes back.

"Which way to town?"

"North. Seven miles."

"If you give me your address, I'll see that these are returned," I say, bowing to his clothes.

"No need to do that," he says, staring at the large front pockets of his gray flannel shirt.

Here it comes, I think, then shrug. From the point of view of eternity, what's one man more or less?

"Consider it an early Christmas present," he says.

"Christmas. Right. Thanks." I walk to the front door, turn around. "And for the coffee. And the bed."

He doesn't move, just nods.

When I get to the end of the driveway, my socks already soaking wet, I look back. He is standing in the doorway, a toothpick in his mouth, the fingers of one hand in the front pocket of his pants. "You won't get very far in this snow dressed like that."

"I'll take my chances."

"You're pretty independent," he says, "for somebody with un-combed hair, no coat, and unless you're hiding it somewhere I don't know about, no money."

I look down at my feet. "No shoes," I say. "You forgot, no shoes."

"The way I figure it, there's two things I could do."

"I know one."

"I could take you back to the highway. Or . . ."

Here it comes.

"Give you a job."

"What's the job?"

"You good with your hands?"

"Some people seem to think so. What did you have in mind?"

"There's a loft out there needs fixing," he says, nodding toward the barn. "I'd do it myself but I have a bad back."

"What's the pay?"

"Free room and board, a few bucks."

I nod my head knowingly. "And I get to screw the boss."

He looks at me as if imagining some act you could only ask a stranger for. I consider how far I would get if I started to run.

"No fringe benefits," he says.

Pigs are among the homeliest of animals, second only to aardvarks and armadillos—the sly smiling slit of a mouth buried beneath the rude snout, two black holes not quite deep enough for fingers; watery eyes, ashamed at the thick crude skull that thickens to the swollen body without relief, except for the large stupid ears; no graceful line of distinction in this embodiment of filth, even the simple twist of the tail is the punchline of a dirty joke.

I'm staring up from the mud at the underbelly of a pig, feeling the wetness seep into the back of my shirt, stick to my skin. I pick myself up out of the wallow, wondering if pigs attack humans. I remember reading somewhere once that they eat their young. Perhaps it's this that limits my sympathy, or maybe it's the eyes, too human in the hulking head and obscene body, as if a sculptor had set out to depict a failed human life, each feature the mark of a specific loss, and left only the eyes to bear witness.

"How's it going?" he asks, standing in the double doorway of the barn, looking up at me. The late afternoon light makes a halo for the dark hair, shadows where his eyes should be.

"Bad."

I am once more balanced on my back on top of the ladder, soggy stockinged feet tucked behind one rung, trying to pound a nail into the two-by-four meant to support the platform of the loft. Beneath me the pigs snort in their own muck, trying to get warm.

"The first nail was too short. The second one was long enough but too thick—it split the two-by-four halfway down. Then I fell off the ladder. Into *that*," I say, pointing to the half-frozen mud or worse.

"If it was easy, they'd let girls do it."

I give him a drop-dead look. "When I want your opinion I'll beat it out of you," I say, pounding the nail in perfectly.

He laughs. "Here," he says, "I brought you some boots and a jacket." He holds them out. "If the boots are too big you can always wear another pair of my socks."

"Who was your charity case this time last year?" I ask, immediately wishing I'd kept the nails in my mouth.

He looks as if somebody had slapped him, sets the boots and socks slowly down, lays the jacket on top, then turns and walks toward the house. I watch him go, upside down, an odd perspective. He moves as if he were proud of having a human body.

When I come into the house an hour later, I'm wearing the clean socks, the boots, and the jacket; my way of saying I'm sorry, but he isn't listening.

"Job's done," I say cheerfully, blowing on my hands. "Got a towel I can use to take a shower?"

"In the closet at the end of the hall," he says in a monotone of indifference, not looking up from the newspaper he's reading at the kitchen table.

In this manner a tenuous living arrangement was made. I did the jobs he requested. After the loft I patched all the holes in the barn to keep the snow out. Then I put a new shingle roof on the shed, where I found boxes of old mildewed books, which I'd read or not read at night in the half-moon light of the tall brass lamp when he'd go into town. *Things of This World. The Far Field.* Poetry mostly. Some history. No philosophy.

He never asked me to cook. Or do dishes. For which I was grateful.

"Take what you need," he said, putting money in the drawer by the kitchen sink. I counted it twice the first week—$200 in twenties and tens; then, on Friday, $325—but I left it in the drawer. I figured I'd stay until New Year's—two weeks away—then take a couple of hundred and buy a bus ticket to wherever I'd decided by then I was going. Dubuque was not a place I'd ever wanted to visit, much less live. Much less with a touchy pig farmer. I knew the type: tall, dark, and lonesome. But he'd kept his word—no fringe benefits. And in this respect he was like no man I had ever met.

A silver package lay on the nightstand beside the bed.

He must have come into the room while I slept. He must have watched me sleep. I feel violated, unclean, have always disliked the idea of someone looking at me when I can't look back. It's one of the reasons I want to be cremated. Scatter the ashes. Let them look at that.

I sit up in bed, light a cigarette, notice the small white card. *Merry Christmas.*

I have always hated Christmas, even before Santa Claus was dead: the attempt to bully goodness by appealing to greed; strange aunts who smothered you in powdered breasts and brought divinity cut in large sickening squares, required eating; the excruciating wait that ended with pretty paper in the fire, the best present; the day my father left, went out for breakfast and never came back.

Isn't it just like a bad movie, I thought, staring out at the snow-covered trees.

Then, too, a present had lain by the bed.

Give the gift of hindsight. But where were the clues? His books and clothes were gone from the house before New Year's—my mother's doing—his face burned out of all the pictures in the photograph album in the cedar chest. How many cigarettes had it taken, I wondered, to make of this man a walking wound? What rage or grief? I'd touched the places where his face had been, the ash coming off on my hands. Gone, gone, as if I had fathered myself and invented a likely past.

Every Christmas I try to reconstruct it, going over the features like a blind person—the fine dark hair that fell over his forehead in a shock, black on pale; blue eyes with flecks of gold in the irises; the straight thin nose that gave his face its insolence, its pride; full lips like a woman's; then the cleft in the chin that had seemed to deepen as the day went.

I was the only one in the family who hadn't gotten it—that deep cleft. "Touched by God," my mother always said. I was not touched by God. "We ran out when we got to you." That was my father's line, making the loss less a matter of grace, more of chance. He didn't believe in God, believed only in human stupidity, taking every instance of it as a personal assault, as if a better possible world actually existed, this one made intolerable by comparison. "Crazy fool," he would mutter, "crazy fool," shaking his head, and for years I had thought it one word: *craziful.*

"There are some folks bound to regard the world with a dark eye," my mother would say. "Your father gets the prize." She the optimist or the pessimist, depending on your view, what you expected. "Too good," she would say with sweet disdain. "He thinks he's too good for this world." A sneer of her own. "Quit every decent job he ever had. And me with three little ones."

When our father had gone, she would lecture us kids—my sister Ellen, my brother David, and me. "Don't kill yourself trying to get your elbow in your ear, it won't fit. There's no more light than what light there is."

I see her now, a small failed woman with a look of intense concentration, focused somewhere in the past. What did she think when she knew for certain that he wasn't coming back? Good morning, good-bye. What story do you tell yourself about that?

"Maybe he didn't like the way I fixed his eggs," she said once, laughing, standing there in front of the heavy black skillet, her hair going gray under a tight bandanna, one hand on her hip, fingers back, staring into the yolks of the eggs, watching them harden, then burn, the smoke rising high in the yellow kitchen.

Maybe. The word's a thumbscrew.

There's a knock at the door. "You going to sleep all day?" Lucky asks.

"Be out in a minute," I say, standing up, stretching, wondering what's in the box, the silver box no longer there on the nightstand, gone, I must've imagined it.

"Lazybones," he says when I come into the kitchen, sit down at the round oak table, cross my arms, put my chin on my wrists.

"New snow," he says, looking out the window over the kitchen sink. "Isn't it beautiful?"

Cheerful son of a bitch.

"You change your mind about breakfast? There's plenty here for both of us. A person should eat a good breakfast. At least on Christmas morning."

I decide to let the irony pass. "No. Thank you."

"You're getting skinny," he says. "Downright scrawny. You better eat."

"It's the clothes," I say, looking down at the Levi's rolled up three times at the cuffs, cinched in at the waist with one of his belts; the plaid wool shirt several sizes too large.

"There's something for you in there under the tree. Open it while you watch me eat."

I go into the living room. With the drapes undrawn, it's dark, except for the colored lights, and I imagine all the possibilities of grief in these bright unknown objects. I get the box from under the tree—wrapped in red foil, not silver—and bring it back to the kitchen table.

"Open it," he says, making his eyes wide like a little kid's.

I open the present slowly, pull the tape off with care, trying not to tear the paper. It's a red long-sleeved cable-knit pullover, black pants, lacy black underwear. I hold them up, raise an eyebrow.

"Don't worry," he says. "Kathleen picked them out. Do you like it?"

"Why are you so good to me?"

"You're cheap labor," he says. "And besides, I'm getting used to having you around."

"Who's Kathleen?"

"Kathleen Evans. You'll meet her this evening. I've invited a couple of people over for Christmas dinner."

The lover, I think. "Does she know about me?"

"Sure."

"What did you tell her?"

"The truth. That you're my hired hand. What else?"

I feel something flare inside, go out, tell myself it's just curiosity. What sort of woman would pick out black underwear for the woman who's living with her lover?

I whistle. "What a spread." The counter is laid with turkey, dressing, cranberry sauce, mashed potatoes, gravy, baked ham, sweet potatoes with brown sugar and marshmallows on top, green beans with bits of bacon, hot rolls, fruit salad, green salad, and two kinds of pie—mince and pumpkin.

"Ham lamb chicken ram turkey hog dog frog, everything but rabbit, squirrel, and black-eyed peas, y'all," he says, doing a little soft-shoe.

I laugh, take the glass of eggnog laced with rum that he holds out to me.

"Don't you look fine in your new duds," he says, raising his glass. "Merry Christmas."

The doorbell rings and he goes to answer it, his head nearly touching the top of the doorframe as he walks through the doorway. I follow him out.

"Kathleen, I'd like you to meet Jesse . . ."

"Walker. Hi."

"Pleased to meet you," Kathleen says and looks genuinely pleased.

A short bald man with close-set eyes comes up the walk, stamps his rubber boots on the front steps, then falls through the door.

"That's Earl down there," Lucky says, laughing. He picks him up, sets him inside the door. "Been hitting it already, huh, Earl?"

"I simply lost my footing," Earl says.

"Earl Sweet, Jesse Walker."

Earl wipes off his hand, wet with snow, and holds it out. "Hello."

"Let me hang those up for you," Lucky says, taking their coats and throwing them in a chair. "Now. What can I get you? Kathleen?"

"A little white wine, sweetie. If you've got it."

"Whiskey," Earl says.

"The man wants *whissskey*," Lucky says, whistling the word.

"Well," Kathleen says, turning to me as soon as Lucky has left the room. "How are you *doing*? Lucky said you'd been in some kind of *accident*." Her eyes pop like Olive Oyl's when she speaks.

"I'm fine now. Can't say the same for the car."

"Well, even *so,* I never could see how anyone could *hitch*hike. It must take a lot of, well, *courage,* I guess. I mean, you never know *who's* going to pick you up, *what* they might take it into their heads to . . ."

"There's a difference between courage and stupidity," Earl says.

"That's what my brother always said."

"What's that?" Lucky asks, bringing in the drinks.

"We were just discussing the difference between courage and stupidity," Earl says.

"Here," Lucky says. "This'll give you a little of both."

"It's courage if you succeed, stupidity if you don't," Earl says, raising his glass. "To success."

"That's what I told myself when I bought this pig farm," Lucky says. "And it didn't make me feel any better knowing it."

"What did you do before that?" I ask, realizing for the first time that he didn't just come into existence for my benefit that morning on the highway.

"New York, nine-to-five, pinstripe suit, working for some half-assed publisher who specialized in dead-cat books."

"A learned man. We have here a learned man," Earl says. Then he turns his little beady bloodshot eyes on me. "What do you do?"

"Didn't he tell you? I'm his hired hand."

"Before this, I mean. What was your line of work before this?"

"Oh. I don't know. Traveled around a lot, I guess."

"A woman of mystery," Earl says.

"No. I just could never keep a job. What about you?"

"Earl tends bar down at the Crazy Horse. Builds the best Long Island tea you ever tasted."

"They call it Texas tea where I come from," I say.

"Where's *that?*" Kathleen asks.

Earl looks at her like she's too dumb to live. "Texas," he says.

"I knew that. I *knew* that. I was only kidding. To anyone else that would have been perfectly obvious."

"Kathleen tears tickets down at the Fox," Earl says. "In case you were wondering how she exercises her, ah, intelligence."

"I'm not so dumb I don't know an *in*sult when I hear one," Kathleen says, drawing herself up to an unimpressive height. "I hope you've got a nice warm place to *sleep* tonight, Earl."

So it's Kathleen and Earl.

"It's Christmas," Lucky says. "Peace on earth, good will, and all that."

"I'm sorry," Earl says. "Truly. Forgive me, Katie?"

Kathleen rolls her green eyes, puts a manicured fingernail to her cheek, and appears to be considering the possibility. "All right," she says finally. "*I* guess. In the spirit of Christmas."

"Well, we've got the names and occupations straight," Lucky says. "Let's eat."

When we are all seated at the kitchen table, our plates filled with more food than anyone could eat, Lucky bows his head, folds his hands under his chin, closes his eyes. "Somebody say grace."

It's what my father used to say. "Grace," I say, and Lucky smiles like this is the right answer to every question he'd ever asked.

"Let's play strip poker," Kathleen says when the table is cleared.

"An old Christmas tradition," Earl says, jerking a thumb at Kathleen.

"Have you got any better ideas?"

"Yes. We could just sit here quietly, watching the snow fall, remembering old times."

"Like the time all you got in your Christmas stocking was an *orange*? No thanks. I'd rather see Lucky naked."

"I thought we'd listen to a little music," Lucky says and puts on Willie Nelson singing "Pretty Paper."

"Cryin' and dyin' music," I say. "Just right for Christmas."

"That was the year I was seven," Earl says. "Or was it eight? Anyway, it was a bad year for farmers because of the drought, and Daddy said I'd be lucky if I got an empty box with a bowribbon on it. Mama said it builds a person's character to go without now and then."

"Depends on what sort of character you're aiming at," Kathleen says, running a hand over her breast and down her right thigh.

Earl ignores it. "May I continue?" he asks with an aggrieved look.

Kathleen slumps on the couch, closes her eyes, sighs deeply, pretends to sleep.

Lucky looks at me above their heads and winks.

"Well, anyway—as I was saying when I was so rudely interrupted—I was seven or eight at the time. It was a bad year for farmers . . ."

It was after midnight when Kathleen and Earl left.

"They really go at each other, don't they?"

"It's not serious," Lucky says.

"He treats her like she's a moron."

"People have their own ways of getting along. Better not to make it too political. Kathleen likes playing the dumb broad."

The way you like playing the dumb pig farmer, I think. "I don't like to hear women called *dumb broads.*"

"What would you call her?"

I consider this a moment. "Not too bright."

"Oh, that's much more polite. I'll tell her the next time I see her. Kathleen, you're not too bright but you are not, by any means, a dumb broad." He snuffles into the top of his beer bottle.

"I was beginning to like you."

"And now that we disagree, you don't."

"You're not as easygoing as you act."

"No. And you're not as tough as you pretend."

"Well, I'll be leaving soon," I say, standing up, setting the empty glass down hard on the coffee table. "And then you won't have to put up with it."

He gives me a one-beer salute and says, "Don't let the door hit you in the ass on the way out."

I have a talent for leaving. I'm not especially fond of those traveling-man songs that make a breast-beating virtue of it (*Baby, Baby, don't get hooked on me. Look out your window, I'll be* . . . Always a man going and some goddamn weeping woman hanging at his knees) but I have been one acquainted with the temptation to move on. If you've ever left somewhere in the middle of a night too cold to put a foot on the floor without whimpering, come home one twilight from a soul-selling job and called the landlady to say she could keep the deposit and the furniture, found yourself heading west on Interstate 90 when the only direction you had in mind was *long gone,* then you know what I mean.

I'm not saying it's easy. Running away, maybe, but not moving on. There are rules for running away. A motive and a point of departure. Moving on requires an act of pure imagination. It's a card game without cards, sleight of hand in an empty theater; no way to count your losses, no applause. Except spatially, running away bears no relation to moving on.

I know when to leave—the precise point beyond which a person is not a person and becomes a dancing dog. Did you hear about that slave-wage DJ down in Austin who locked herself in the sound room and played "Take This Job and Shove It" for three and a half hours until the big boss came with the key and the police? That's only the most dramatic exit. I've quit so many jobs my résumé is a study in geography. But the real test of a talent for leaving is leaving a man. Love is litmus; in the metaphysics of farewell, the final exam.

The only thing I took when I left my husband was a vow of promiscuity. I thought I knew all about traveling light. My favorite line from a movie was *I don't stop for nothin', honey, but I slowed down for you.* It is better to have loved and lost. Speak softly and carry a passport. When you're leaving you're already gone.

I knew by the way my hands lingered on the objects in the borrowed room that I wouldn't go. New Year's Day came and went. We shared a hangover. I said a hangover is not the proper point of view for beginning a journey. I said it was because I couldn't take his money, but it wasn't that.

The body remembers every extraordinary kindness, makes its own allies . . .

It was one of those nights—walking through my life as if it were a train station, my mind an empty suitcase. No, more like this. Driving along in my car once, my ghetto blaster beside me, I slipped in a homemade Judy Collins tape, turned it on; only I pushed *Record* by mistake, and the first half of "The Moon Is a Harsh Mistress" was erased. Playing it back, there was nothing but the sound of the machine recording its own noise, a senseless roaring sound.

I had gone to take a shower, hoping something would come to me—in the pattern of the tile, the texture of the thick blue towel, a memory of water. I let the hot water beat on my skin for a long time, then got out, wiped the steam from the full-length mirror on the back of the door, stood staring at the portrait of the stranger in glass.

He walked in on me like that. "I'm sorry," he said, backing up. "I didn't know . . ."

"It doesn't matter. It's only a body."

He closed the door, came toward me, put his hands on my shoulders, looked down. I didn't move. Then I saw, in the mirror, him kneeling, his mouth on my breast, while I leaned slightly forward, my knees on his knees, felt his hands grip the backs of my thighs. He lay down, and I watched the woman in the mirror unbutton his shirt, undo his belt with one hand, unzip his pants, pull them lower; watched as her mouth found its way down his chest, her wet hair on his belly, down. He cried out and I quieted him, "Shh, shh," wondering who the woman, why this man, why here on the dark blue linoleum still damp.

He picked me up and carried me into the bedroom, laid me down on the bed. My body was still wet from the shower and it tingled where the cool air moved over it. He touched my breasts where the cool air had been, the insides of my arms, my palms. "Pretty pretty," he said. I tried to touch him but he moved my hand away. "This one's on me," he said, getting up from the bed, looking down at me. He smiled, took off his shirt and his socks—all that was left—and his cock rose stiff in the air, as if some strange and lovely bird. He lay beside me, watched my face, as his fingers touched one nipple then the other. There was a heaviness, a pulsebeat between my legs, and I tried to move his hand lower but he wouldn't be hurried. "Not yet," he said, taking a nipple between his teeth, biting gently, flicking it with his tongue, now the other, as if time were all he had, as if this were not prologue but a long meditation on pleasure.

A quarter moon cut my thigh, lay on the dark blue cover, and he touched me where the light entered. Slowly, gently, as if something of great importance depended on this slow and steady pleading of hands. "Is this what you want? Is this it?" he asked, and when I didn't answer he stopped. The absence of pleasure seemed an assault. "Yes." He began again, his mouth then, his fingers filling me up while his tongue moved over the small hard bead of skin, the pleasure coming from too many sources for the body to understand. He straddled me then, his mouth taking turns with my breasts, holding them high and taut, the nipples like hard candy. He let his cock dangle between my legs, and I lifted my hips, rubbed against him, but he raised up, away, went on with my breasts, holding my arms above my head, against the pillow. I raised my hips as high as I could, to the ceiling it seemed, but only the tip was in, only the tip. "I want." "What do you want? "I *want*..." "What? Say it." "I want you inside me." Already at the edge, one simple thrust put me over but he didn't stop. He moved my hands down to my sides, held the wrists tightly, watching my face, every outward movement a loss. Another wave hit and I felt my body heave and tremble, my thighs grab and heave, then he put my legs around his neck to bring him deeper, so deep I thought I would drown. I was crying then, surprising sobs. "Am I hurting you? I don't want to hurt you." "No," I said, wiping the sweat from his face, suddenly dear, but he took my legs from his shoulders and turned me gently over. I raised up on my knees, felt his thighs tight against me, his hand on his cock, guiding it in. He began again, the slow and steady movements that made me think pleasure had an exact and single rhythm. "I've wanted to do this since the first day," he said. "Before then." I lay my wet face on the pillow, gripped the pillow with both hands, pressed against him, and we came together with such force that my bones ached and I wondered at the difference between pleasure and pain—then he let go, a sound like grief ripped from him. We trembled together, fell still, the substantial weight of him against my back, his open mouth on my neck; stayed wrapped like that for what seemed a night, then he took himself gently away, lay by my side, held my face in his hands and kissed me. "Oh sweetie," he said. "Oh sweetie." As if the woman were a child, wakened from a bad dream, and only this rocking could soothe her. "Never," I whispered, meaning what? Never again? Never like this? "I'm gone," he said. "I'm a goner." Then he laughed, and I remembered that this was a particular man, with a history of his own, and a face I must see in the morning. "I don't love you," I told him, so there would be no mistake.

But the body has reasons that reason itself knows nothing of. And in the morning this world will seem certain, necessary, as if a long line of argument had led to this place with the inevitability of deduction.

He will look at me with sympathy or regret, quiet as usual but deeper drawn, his eyes avoiding my eyes, like a child caught staring, conscious of his hands.

"Only a night," I will say, "only a night. It doesn't matter."

"It matters," he will say, getting up, taking my face in his hands. Then he will make me breakfast and I will eat it, the last breakfast, only hand and mouth away from saying it: yes, it matters, yes, because one cannot live from the point of view of eternity.

PART TWO

The Far Field

The house was tight against the snow that winter, snow as deep as a grave, making it difficult to imagine what lay under it, or where, even if one knew, to draw the border between Lucky's farm and the neighbors'—Amelia Salmon, a widow, to the west, and to the east the Burgesses, a family of five, faces I never saw—the endless white on white making the distance between here and anywhere seem greater.

In the early mornings we would lie in bed trying to devise new ways of fairly deciding who would get up first to build the fire, make the coffee. Scissors, paper, rock. I am thinking of an object . . . Hangman played in the dust on the nightstand. When I lost I was glad. There is a sense of possession in building a fire in the house before anyone is up—the laying of kindling and crumpled newspaper, the first easy blaze, then carrying the heavy logs in from the porch to the grate, watching them catch and blacken—a sense of possession and being possessed: by the sudden warmth on your hands, your face, that particular blue at the center of the flame.

While I waited for the water to boil for coffee, I would set out two thick white cups on a wooden tray, with silver spoons, milk, and sugar. At such times I thought my life made sense, here at the center of these ordinary objects. For a congenital malcontent it seemed almost shocking to admit: I was happy.

I wanted to tell someone.

I thought of calling Torrie but I knew what she would say: "A pig farmer? You're in love with a *pig* farmer?" I could hear her snorting laughter. "Never take a pig farmer out to dinner. You can dress him up but you can't teach him to eat." She had a putdown for every man I'd ever told her I loved. We'd been friends for sixteen years but the way things were now could not be entrusted to her.

I thought of calling my mother in California, someone I talked to or visited only in times of grief. I don't know why that was; perhaps because she herself seemed only fit for grief, as if any chance at happiness would be threatened with disbelief, doubted, stared down until it died. And I could not imagine the words forming in my mouth, what I would say. "Hi Mom. The screaming inside my head hasn't stopped but it's quieter."

Then it occurred to me why I wouldn't call. To tell it would be to make it real, something independent of me, something that could be lost. I never called anyone. And I began to think of Lucky as outside my ordinary life, the long line of leave-takings, changes of heart, lost selves.

When the coffee was ready, I'd carry the tray down the hall, noting each creak and whine of the floorboards, deftly avoiding splinters, a nail slightly raised, as if such knowledge constituted ownership. And Lucky would be where he had been, his dark hair nearly black against the white pillow, his farmer's tan dividing his body, making him seem like two different men.

Except for feeding the pigs, which we did after breakfast, the days were our own. Lucky would tinker with an old Jaguar he had parked beneath the loft in the barn, a '54 XK 120 drophead coupe with red leather interior. He spent hours tuning the engine, refinishing the teak dashboard, sanding down the body of the car and having it repainted—seventeen coats of white, shining the hood ornament. When I told him he treated that car as if it were a work of art, he said, "It is." He told me a story then about a man in Dallas, Texas, who owned a Jaguar—how he came out of his house one morning and saw a kid of about sixteen sitting in the driver's seat; the man went back into the house, got a gun, and shot the kid. The kid didn't die, but Lucky laughed when he told the story, and it made me wonder whether I knew him, whether this wasn't just the sort of detail the grief-stricken family of the ax man's victim would seize upon later as prophetic, as if the difference between paranoia and realism were only a matter of time.

While Lucky was working on the car, I chopped the wood under the lean-to behind the house and otherwise spent my time fixing things. I put new hinges on the double doors of the barn so they closed all the way and kept the wind and snow out. I laid a new linoleum floor in the kitchen—dark blue—and painted the walls and high ceilings white. With the help of a rented sander I stripped the floor in the living room down to bare wood, smooth and white, then stained it a light shade of oak, and spent one whole day rubbing paste wax into it.

One afternoon in February, before the snow began to melt, Lucky got the rusted yellow Caterpillar started up and drove it out over the back field, me beside him on the rig. Everything was cold and white and we were high up in the world, arctic explorers on some giant metal insect, looking down on a settlement of snow, the rolling of the Caterpillar rocking us. I tried to tell him something, how familiar it seemed, déjà vu, but the roar of the Caterpillar's engine was louder than my voice. He turned to me then and, seeing my lips move I guess, turned off the key. When the trembling of the engine had subsided, everything was quiet. "What, Jesse? What did you say?" I could feel the cold smooth material of his parka against my face, the warmth of his breath, his solid body against mine, and I couldn't say anything.

Geese, I have read, will bond with the first thing they see after birth—whether it's mother goose, human, or rubber boot—and will follow it anywhere. I have sometimes wondered if humans are different, or if we too are moved by what we cannot remember. Maybe it was the land, reminding me of the place where I grew up in the San Joaquin Valley, or the way he dressed—plaid wool shirts, Levi's, boots—a familiar gesture of consolation or disgust, some reticence of response, or it may have been his hair, black as burnt wood, or the dark blue eyes so like my father's, but whatever the reason, I knew my heart was in my mouth too much of the time, that it was getting harder and harder to walk away, even in my imagination.

In the afternoons we often took long walks to the farthest edge of the land and back, all bundled up in down and mittens, the sun bright on the snow, making us squint. It was on these walks that I tried, without much success, to get Lucky to tell me about himself.

"Have you lived here a long time?" I asked at the beginning, deciding to start on the easy questions first and work up to the ones about the meaning of life.

"Going on five years," he said. He looked down at his boots. "Yep. Bought these here shitkickers just about five years ago."

I laughed. "What did you wear before that—wing tips?"

"How'd you guess?"

"Somehow it's hard to imagine you in a suit—a stuffed shirt with a blue pen."

"I used a red pen," he said.

I laughed. "What'd you do before that?"

He looked at me like this was classified information and I didn't have a clearance. "I was a commodities broker," he said finally.

"What's that?"

"You take orders from people for stuff they don't want—pork bellies, wheat, gold—and hope the price goes down or up, depending on whether they sold short or long, and when it doesn't you get sued for your efforts. Futures, it's called."

"Futures. How long did you do that?"

"Long enough to lose my ass. That's enough about me," he said abruptly. "What did you do before I met you? I know you had to earn a living somehow. Unless you're independently wealthy and keeping it a secret."

"I did a lot of things," I said. "Most of them shit jobs."

"Like what?" He was better at asking questions than at answering them, I noticed.

"I played the piano in a place called Ivy's in Bacliff, Texas, a few years back. With Peewee Wilson on steel guitar and Iris Long on drums. I wonder whatever happened to Peewee and Iris. That was one job I liked."

"Do you still know how to play?"

"Oh, I'm pretty rusty. I wasn't that good to start with." I thought of my mother, cutting up apples to explain what a quarter note, a half note, and an eighth note were, before I could read.

"What else?"

"I tended bar in a place called the Red Dog Saloon in Juneau, Alaska. That was, let's see . . . seven years ago. Jesus. I'm getting old. There was a woman who sang there on Friday and Saturday nights who sounded like Phoebe Snow. A voice that could break your heart."

"I've always wanted to go to Alaska," Lucky said, staring off across the field of snow as if he could see it. "Land of the Midnight Sun."

"It was. In the summer it stayed daylight until eleven-thirty, twelve at night. I had to put tinfoil over the windows so I could get some sleep. But I loved it there. There was a spirit I haven't found anywhere else, of . . . I don't know . . . the sense that you could walk out the front door and change your life." We were at the edge of the land and we both turned back toward the house at the same time, as if we had been walking this trail all our lives.

"Why'd you leave?" he asked then.

"It's a long story. You don't want to hear it."

"I do."

"I don't want to tell it. I think there should be a statute of limitations on sad stories."

We walked for a while in silence. Then, to make up for holding something back, I told him something else I was ashamed of. "After that I went home. Home to my mother," I said, shaking my head. "Got a job packing peaches at $1.75 an hour." I talked without looking at him. "That lasted about three weeks. I couldn't stand the feel of the fuzz on my hands." I laughed, as if telling about somebody else's life that hadn't worked out.

"A woman of many talents," he said, but I could tell that the space between us had subtly changed, widened. Still, there was nothing to do except act like it hadn't.

"After that, let's see . . . I was an oyster shucker at a little place in New Orleans. I forget the name. Bob's Oyster Bar, I think. I quit that job when I almost cut my left thumb off." I pulled off my glove and held out my hand to show him the long thin scar.

"Poor baby," he said and kissed the skin between my forefinger and thumb.

I just kept talking, trying to act nonchalant, as if I could still breathe. "Then I sold, or I should say *tried* to sell, home satellite dishes to strangers over the telephone. Told them they could pick up signals from the moon. Three hundred and forty-six stations. All sports and sitcoms. Whatever they wanted. At that job I lasted exactly two days. People kept hanging up on me and I'd end up crying."

He laughed. "What were you doing that landed you on the side of I-90 where I found you?"

"I wrote obituaries," I said. "For a newspaper in New Hampshire. That lasted almost a year."

"Obituaries?"

"You know. Those little columns with the dead person's name in caps at the top, with their dubious achievements and those dearly beloved left behind?" Against my will I imagined my own obituary—JESSE WALKER, 35—with Lucky Redbord as the husband left to grieve. So young, so much to live for. Then I pictured another scene: me getting into a sports car, putting the top down, slipping my best leaving-town tape into the tape deck, gunning the engine, heading west, singing: *Like a bird on the wire, like a drunk in a midnight choir, I have tried, in my way, to be free* . . .

"I know what an obituary is," Lucky said. "I just didn't think anybody did that for a living. Just that, I mean."

"You're looking at her."

"I like the way it looks," he said, and everything came right again; we were equal—either both drowning or both saved.

"So far," I said. "Give yourself a chance."

"I'll do that." He took my hand, and we walked for a while without talking.

"What are you going to be when you grow up?"

"That's what I keep asking myself. I'm no spring chicken, as my mother would say. I'll be thirty-five next December. The same age my father was when he . . . said adios. Some days I worry about it. Then other days I think, who's watching, who's keeping score? You know?"

"You had a birthday while you were here and you didn't tell me?" He shook his head and wagged his finger as at a wayward child.

"It was the first night. I didn't know you well enough then to ask for what I wanted."

"Well, we're going to have to rectify that," he said. "Have a little belated celebration."

When I came into the kitchen that evening after cleaning out the shed, he was frying chicken in the big black skillet. There were small new potatoes in a pan, a glass bowl of chocolate pudding cooling on the table, and in a large blue bowl were pear slices, Queen Anne cherries, white grapes, fresh strawberries, figs. In the center of the table was a chocolate cake with dark chocolate frosting.

"Looks good," I said, thinking how nice it is to have a man cook for you.

"There's a scene in the movie *Tom Jones,*" Lucky said, "where the hero and the wench eat supper together, each at one end of a long table that's laid out with food. For your dining pleasure this evening, I'm going to do my best to reproduce it." Here he did a little tap dance and presented the table with both hands. "Ta-*da*!"

"You're the hero and I'm the wench, I suppose."

"You catch on very quickly."

I got a spoon out of the drawer and tasted the chocolate pudding. "Mmm."

"No silverware," he said. "At this supper you can only use your hands." He touched my breast to demonstrate, then went back to tending his chicken.

"How do you eat pudding with your hands?"

"Like this," he said, dipping his middle finger into the pudding then putting it in my mouth. "But you really should wait for the whipped cream."

"When's supper?" I asked. "Do I have time for a shower?"

"If you hurry. The chicken's almost ready. We should eat right away if you want it hot."

"I do."

I was happy in that house, happier than I ever want to be again, the kind of happiness that is half magic, half fear of annihilation.

When the isolation made us strange, even to ourselves, we would call up Earl and Kathleen to go out dancing and drinking. There was a place we invariably ended up, the Stoneleigh P. It used to be a pharmacy but the letters fell off and they made it a bar. There's a moral there somewhere, but what? Windows along one wall—ceiling to floor—that looked out on the Mississippi. Hot Polish sausage when it got too late for dinner. Patsy Cline and Jim Reeves on the jukebox. If we went on a Saturday night, there would be a band named Heart Trouble with a blind lead singer who sounded like Jessi Colter. She had to be led onto the stage, but when you heard her sing you thought seeing didn't matter.

I remember one Saturday night, because it taught me something about myself that I didn't want to know.

We'd planned to meet Earl and Kathleen at the Stoneleigh P around nine. Lucky and I got there at quarter after, already half sloshed, having started earlier at a place called Marie's, a little dive on the south side of town that played Spanish love songs on the jukebox.

We stumbled across the dark parking lot, following the light of the Coors sign toward the bar, walked in, looked around. No sign of

Earl or Kathleen, so we sat down at a table in the corner and ordered two Scotch and waters, waiting for the music to start.

I sometimes thought that I could learn something important about my life from the times I'd changed drinks. First it was sloe gin and Seven-Up, in high school. Then Seagram's VO. Next came boiler-makers, the years of revolution and self-destruction. White wine for a while, an attempt to be ladylike, moderate. Then Cuba libres, purposely low class. Now Scotch and water. It always signaled a radical change, and if I took the trouble to think about it, I might have figured something out. But this was a thought I usually had while drinking one of those drinks, so it didn't have much chance to develop.

"Here's to the best winter of my life," Lucky said, raising his glass to me.

"Really? You're not kidding?"

"Hell no. I wouldn't kid about a thing like that."

"That's nice. That's really nice. Nobody ever said anything like that to me before." Hell to live with was, until then, the consensus.

"Haven't you been happy? Haven't we been happy together?"

I thought of the breath held at the top of the roller coaster's sharpest descent. "Yes."

Just then the boys in the band came out, started testing the equipment. "One. Two." The blind singer wasn't up there, and I wondered what happened to her. After the introductions, they began with a little warmup tune called "Whiskey River."

"May I have the pleasure?" Lucky asked, standing up, bowing at the waist, with his left arm straight out, pointing toward the dance floor.

I smiled. A lot of the things he did made me smile.

"How're you doing?" he asked after a while. He was always checking my temperature, seeing if I was all right.

"Good," I said, and he hugged me, lifted me up off the floor and whirled me around. I can remember the exact light in that room, the smoke and the music, his heart pounding against my chest, a second heart, as from inside.

* * *

Earl and Kathleen came in around ten.

"Howdy, stranger," Lucky said to Earl. "Katie. What've you been up to?"

"We're fine, sweetie," Kathleen said, kissing Lucky on the cheek.

Something went off in my head, some kind of alarm that doesn't make a sound. *Sweetie.* I knew that Lucky and Kathleen had been lovers. He'd said the same thing to her that he said to me.

Earl and Kathleen sat down at the table, and I dragged Lucky up for another dance. "Drink up," I said, looking back at them. "We're way ahead of you." Kathleen waved and smiled, nodding her head.

"What right's she got calling you *sweetie,* huh, sweetie?" The band was playing "Your Cheatin' Heart," which I thought was appropriate, and I started to sing along with the music.

"What?"

"Kathleen. Back there. She called you sweetie." I said it like it was a dirty word.

"So? Is there some law against that?" he said, pulling me close, rubbing his cheek against my cheek.

"No. No law," I said, pulling away. "It's just that I thought *I* was the only one you called sweetie, and it makes me think maybe Kathleen and I have something in common," I said, putting my hand where he would understand exactly what I was saying.

"It was a long time ago," he said. "Just something between friends."

"You screw all your friends?"

"No, just the ones who ask for it," he said, smiling, trying to smile me out of being mad. Then, seeing my face not change, he said, "Hell, Jesse. I had a life before you. You knew that."

"You should have told me."

"Why?"

I couldn't think of an answer to that so I didn't say anything.

"Come on, swee— Jess," he said. "Don't be mad."

"I'm not mad. But don't you see, it makes it used."

"If you wanted something brand-new, you came to the wrong

place," he said. "You better get 'em a little younger if that's what you had in mind." He laughed. "Like thirteen."

"Fuck you," I said and walked back to the table.

"Hey," he called after me. "You forgot something."

"Nothing I want," I said, not looking back.

The band had just finished and people were slowly drifting back to their tables. I tried to dodge a guy coming toward me but he kept moving the way I was moving to get around him. When we finally got our sidestepping coordinated, he said, "Thanks for the dance."

I sat down at the table, crossed my arms over my chest, sighed deeply.

"What's with you guys?" Kathleen asked.

"Nothing," I said.

"I guess the honeymoon's over," Earl said. "It's about time. You two were beginning to make me puke."

"Oh, shut up, Earl," I said, not even pretending to be polite. "Shut up, shut up, shut up."

"So good to see *you* again, *too,*" he said brightly.

I laughed. "Sorry." I was sorry. It seemed silly right then, making so much trouble over a word. I didn't know why I'd done it, what it meant.

"Have another drink," Kathleen said. "That'll cheer you up. What're you having? I'll go get it for you."

"Scotch and water," I said. "Thanks."

Lucky came back to the table and sat down beside me. I held myself stiff, stared straight ahead. He put his hand palm down on the table between us. Without looking sideways, I put my hand on top of his.

"Okay," he said.

My heart was beating hard and I could feel my pulse in my neck. It made me scared how much I wanted him.

"Who was your first great love?" I asked Lucky that night when we got home from the Stoneleigh P. The moon was a sliver, our faces and bodies in shadow, only a band of light at the foot of the bed.

"You," he said solemnly. "There was no one before you. Before you I was only *waiting* to live."

"Very funny," I said, elbowing him in the ribs. "Now tell me. Who was she?"

"Jesse," he said. "That's with an *e* on the end. It's important to get the spelling right. Capital *J-e-s-*"

"Okay. Forget it. I can see you're not taking this seriously."

"I'm taking it very seriously. It's just that I can't remember anyone before you. You've dazzled my memory."

Even sulking and sarcasm, my great gifts, got me nowhere. Maybe I had scared him with that little scene at the bar, or maybe he was just discreet, a highly overrated virtue. Whatever the reason was, he would never tell me anything about the women he'd loved before me. Only that he'd been married once, to someone named Annie, and that it had lasted five years, no kids. Not even his tone of voice gave him away. It could have been anything—indifference, love, or grief.

So I had to imagine how it was with Annie and him, what she was like, the way it must have ended. Imagining the real is more difficult than making it up. There is something to be true to.

She would have long hair, I thought. Long, thick, as black as the blackest hair, like Evelyn Delgado's, my best friend in second grade. Her eyes, then, would have to be brown, unless they were black, but black eyes are rare, so brown. Her skin would be dark, exotic, not the fish-pale whiteness of my own. I imagined her here, in this bed, the shadows playing on her face, her breasts, and it made me catch my breath—to think how easily I could be gone.

I began again, resolving to keep my mind on the task: black hair, dark brown eyes. But these were mere physical details, the easiest to get right or wrong. What was she like? Shy and passionate. Unsure that anyone could love her but easily convinced. For a living she . . . taught high school French. *Voulez-vous coucher avec moi ce soir?* This was their private joke. The only French he knew.

No, make her an artist. Painter of huge bright canvases, all slashes of pain and no thought. She'd had several one-woman shows, a modest but loyal following: everyone suffers. She'd left him to . . . Why? Why had she left him?

I ran my hand over his chest, lightly, liking the feel of the coarse dark hairs, the way he moved into my touch, the sense of ownership in its being my right to touch him this way, without permission.

She'd left him to go to New York, I decided, after a new snow fell. By then Lucky was asleep and I pulled the blankets up over him, tucked him in, the way you would a beloved child, as if I would not see him again, as if I were the one who was leaving. How could she be a successful artist in Dubuque? They both knew—she couldn't. That's why they split up. For love of her life's possibilities, for art.

No, that's probably not true. Nothing so evenly matched as love and art. Probably it was only another man, someone inferior to Lucky but who was not so silent, so unforthcoming about his past, who would tell her more of his own free will and not make her beg for details. Someone named Bud, who was medium height, medium intelligence, medium everything. Someone who didn't threaten her with his brooding, sorrowing refusal to speak of it.

He had probably told her more in the truck on the highway that first morning than in the three months since. She tried hard to remember it. His unmarried mother pregnant with him, the father only a night, the lecherous butcher, how he'd gotten his name. His mother left him when he was . . . how old? She couldn't remember. Left him with an aunt and uncle in, let's see, somewhere in Texas . . . Nacogdoches? No. Waxahachie, that was it. His words came back: pinched lips, dead eyes, you know the type—dutiful. Then the mother had gone off in search of the true love she thought she deserved but had not found yet. Did she find it? Yes. Again and again.

No father, abandoned by his mother, raised by mean-spirited puritans. What did that explain? His tenderness, his generosity?

She remembered a trip they'd made once, to Phoenix. He'd wanted to take her to a blues bar he'd been happy at, to hear Sonny Terry and Brownie McGhee. They'd stayed in some one-night-stand motel, plastic glasses, tin ashtrays, thin walls. While they were dressing to go out the first night, they'd heard a child crying in the next room.

"Shut up! Shut the fuck up or I'll give you something to cry about!" The sound of flesh striking flesh, more crying, the pitch higher and louder, wailing, really. "I said shut *up*! Shut your goddamn mouth or we won't be going anywhere!"

"What should we do?" she asked. "Shouldn't we call the police?" She headed toward the phone beside the bed.

"No." It was the fear in his voice that stopped her. He had looked at her with such grief, his face closing in upon itself, the eyes sliding away.

"Why not? Jesus Christ! The kid's being *beaten*!"

"They might come. They might come and split the family up. That would be worse."

Would it? She didn't know. He said it with such authority.

"And when they opened the door, the kids would be sitting on the edge of the bed with their red raw faces wiped clean. And they would sit quietly, the way their mother said, because when she beat them she wept. Because if this is how your mother treats you, how would strangers treat you? And because if they showed their pain, their mother would get rid of the police and she would turn on them and it would be *Now* look what you've done! And because even as children they knew that shame was worse than pain." He recited all this as if it were written down somewhere or stored up in his head, brutal poetry.

She went into the bathroom and threw up in the toilet, holding her own head, wiping her mouth with some thin white rag of a washcloth. Sitting on the cold linoleum floor, she looked up at a cheap reproduction of Jesus on the cross above the towel rack, bleeding at the palms but with a beatific look on his face. It seemed as sick as next door, as in this room, to hear a child beaten and not try to stop it.

Soon it was quiet.

She came out of the bathroom feeling weak, shaky, defeated, as if she were the one whose skin was raw. They looked at each other, then looked away, accomplices in something she didn't want to know the name of. Without speaking about the blues bar, they quickly packed the clothes they had just taken out of the suitcase, looked behind them before closing the door, as if this were a place they had lived once and wanted to remember.

The child became the man, and she couldn't stay with him after that. She moved to New York, had some success as an artist. Her paintings were more realistic but they were still about pain, now with great black holes in them, a child's depiction of loss, flowers the color of bruises.

No, that's not why she left. Who knows why anyone leaves? The reasons always come later, when we most need them.

Maybe she just walked out, like a sock in the stomach, taking the air right out of him. Or maybe she operated according to a code that was impossible to decipher unless you knew her, the places she'd been, what the words meant when she said them. Or it might have been something simple, easy to overlook: she wanted him to always remember her and so she left.

I watched him sleeping, tried to become him, but he didn't give me enough to go on, never enough. Like trying to draw a dot-to-dot picture from which half the dots were missing, with a pencil that kept disappearing.

I woke him up then, with my hands. I wanted to make love, wanted to be close to him, to not think for a while—why people did what they did, what would become of us. I ran my hand down his belly, lightly, he might have been dreaming, kissed his shoulder, pressed myself in a curve close to his back.

"Jesse?" he whispered, turning his head slightly, eyes closed, as if even now, these many years later, it might have been her.

Sometimes I took long walks alone into the woods that ran behind Lucky's land. The woods belonged to Hope and Bill Burgess, neighbors, but Lucky said they didn't mind if we walked there. I liked the dark of the trees after the harsh winter light, the blinding snow.

I learned to sit quietly, watching a squirrel size me up quickly then turn its head, dart away for several steps, then pause, as if to reconsider. I had never before taken the time to sit like this, just to look—at the way the snow fell from the heavy branches of pines, as if in benediction, at the slight trembling of the branch just before it fell. I had always been too much in a hurry, and for what? I thought of all the lost days. All the days in which the present was most remarkable for what it did not contain. Now I studied the restless clouds, one whole morning, and I stared until my eyes blurred at the tracks of small animals. I used to be afraid of the cold, but here I sat without feeling it, thinking only of the way the snowbanks converge and the sky whitens after a storm.

I thought of my father who, in woods like these, would bury treasures in a wooden cigar box. There would be pieces of chocolate the shape of coins, covered in gold foil, three silver dollars from a trip to State Line, Lake Tahoe, yellowed pictures of make-believe relatives long dead, a handmade scroll telling of their exploits, their risky adventures and noble deeds, perhaps a message in code with instructions for how to decipher it, trinkets—small charms for a gold bracelet, the Eiffel Tower, Statue of Liberty, cat's eyes, agates, gold rings with large ruby or sapphire stones. He would draw an elaborate map with directions and pictures so we three children might find where the treasure was buried. Take twenty-six steps north, then walk east for forty-two steps, turn around three times, cross the bridge (here was a picture of a fairy-tale bridge) over the creek, go west seventy-seven steps, stop at the oak tree nearest the pond (another picture), dig down three feet for buried TREASURE, the exact spot marked with a red X. The map would be on my nightstand when I got up that morning or on the nightstands of one of the other children, David or Ellen. Where had the map come from? He told us once that he had bid on a box of odds and ends when someone's estate was being sold at auction. It was in the box. It was ours, he said, because we were the ones who understood what was really worth something, while other people bid only on antique furniture or heavy silver or handmade quilts. There was a ring I had saved from one of these treasure hunts, with an expandable gold band, the stone a large sapphire, that had been in a box in the trunk of my car when it crashed. At that moment I wanted it back, felt sick with longing for it.

At the edge of the far field where Lucky's land meets the woods, I stopped to pick up a stone, smooth as the ones I sometimes found at the edge of the sea at Santa Cruz when I was young. It seemed a good omen, not a replacement for the ring but something in kind, and I took it back home with me.

"What was your mother like? Did you hate her for leaving you with people who didn't love you? Have you forgiven her?"

Lucky would smile at me fondly when I began what he called The Inquisition, as if he were above the bad magic of cause and effect that crippled others but knew I couldn't stop asking. "I'm just a simple country boy, nothing hidden," he'd say with elaborate humility, opening the palms of his hands for proof.

I never believed it. Everyone's life was the scene of some terrible accident. And if you didn't know what that accident was, you were just looking for trouble without being able to see it coming.

"What about you?" he asked to throw me off. "Tell me more about your father."

We were sitting at the kitchen table, as we often did in the early evening, drinking Scotch. Drinking the sun down, he called it.

"For all I know, he's dead. I don't wait anymore for him to come back, if that's what you mean. I don't hope for it. I may be slow but I'm not stupid." This always made him smile.

"Where do you think he is now?"

"I don't know. Pago Pago, maybe. He always wanted to go to Pago Pago. Or Australia. Or the Mediterranean. He said once that he wanted to sail every ocean in the world. I suppose he's done it by now."

"Do you miss him?"

"Miss him?" No one had ever asked me this question. I thought about it. I thought of him telling me The One True Story of the World, night after night, then carrying me on his shoulders to bed. He taught me to ride a horse—Slug, we named him, because he was so slow. He let me sit on his lap on the tractor or the harvester when he was working in the field, let me drive the car from our driveway down the gravel road to the highway starting when I was four or five, taught me to steer with one finger, to turn *into* a spin, called me a natural, said I could race stock cars when I grew up if I wanted to. He showed me how to use his tools—plane and hammer and dovetail saw—for the Tahiti ketch he was building in the barn. "I miss him."

"What would you say to him if he came back?"

"Say?"

"Yeah. Isn't there anything you practice over and over in your head? Like, You dirty no-good SOB."

It was such a surprise, his putting it like that, as if he knew, that I told the truth. "Yes."

"What?"

I took a slow sip of Scotch. "When I know you better, maybe I'll tell you."

"Aw, come on." He made a kissing sound, his lips puckered toward me.

"No."

"You want me to beg? I'll beg, if that's what you want." He got down on his knees at my feet, put his hands in praying position, his elbows on my knees, and, with pitiful hangdog eyes, said, "Oh, puh-*lease.*"

"I ask him why he walked out on his life. I ask him if it was because he didn't love us enough."

He laid his head in my lap and I smoothed his hair.

I have a confession to make. You know what it's like: you look into somebody's eyes and see that for him you do not quite exist, your feelings are weightless, your arm a rag arm, your eyes reflect but do not see, your words are something to play back at night so he might have a second chance at a better line than the one he gave you the first time around. You are a straight man, a stock character in his story of the universe, and of course he is the hero, the main event, the author. That's what I was like before I met Lucky.

"Let's go to bed," he said and led me down the dark hall.

"What about your uncle?" I asked when we were propped up against the pillows. "Did he treat you as if you were his son?" There was only enough light left in the room to see the outlines of things.

"He was a do-gooder. If he couldn't convert you, he'd kill you." He laughed. Then he put his fingers through his hair, and I knew he'd thought of something.

"What? Tell me."

He looked at me and even though it was nearly dark I knew what his face looked like.

"I'll make it worth your while," I said, running a hand over my breast.

"Well, my uncle was a religious man, and when I had done something the Lord didn't love—as I did fairly often—he would hold my hand over the flame of a candle."

"Jesus."

"I remember one time I left the barn door open and two calves got out. I chased them down for hours, trying to get the harness on their narrow heads and lead them back to the barn. But their heads were smaller than a horse's and they kept slipping out. I finally got them back in by tightening the harness a couple of notches. When I came into the house, he had the candle already lit, a huge fat one that never burned down. He must've seen me coming, the son of a bitch. I told him I got them back in and locked the barn door tight. I told him I was sorry." Even now, years later, there was fear on his face. "He said, *Sorry* is a useless word. Come over here, son." Lucky's voice was low, melodramatic. "He held my hand at the wrist over the fire until I screamed like a little girl. To teach me a lesson, is what he said." Lucky laughed, squinted his eyes as if trying to see something, shook his head. "I never knew what that lesson was, except maybe that human flesh burns."

I touched his hand, carefully, as if it might still be hot. "Do you hate him?"

"No. Hate is too clean a word for what I feel for that bastard." He wrung an imaginary neck.

"What about your aunt? Was she nice to you?"

"Sure. Nice as pie," he said and then reached for me. "Enough of the past, sweetie. How about a little of the present." He got up and lit the candle on the dresser, then lay back down beside me, unbuttoned the top three buttons of my shirt, put both hands around my waist,. pulled me up onto his lap, facing him, and kissed my breasts. I unbuttoned the rest of the buttons, took off the shirt. "I want you," he said, looking straight into my eyes, squinting, as if it were a puzzle even to him, "I want you," rolling me onto my back, a knee on either side of my thighs, unbuttoning the top button of my pants, breathing erratically, "I really want you," the zipper sticking, him yanking it, "Hurry," as if sex were not only pleasure but consolation and forgetting.

"Wait," I said, feeling left way behind, suddenly scared, and he slowed everything down, put his head on my chest, rested it there, and I wondered if he could feel my heart beating inside his head.

"I love you," he said after a while, and I tried to memorize everything, the pattern of shadows in the room, the covers carelessly thrown, the candle on the dresser, its flame erratic, dancing, but he was kissing me again, my face, my hands, my breasts, teasing my thighs with his tongue, touching me lightly, making me wait, and when I was only this wanting he put his tongue inside me, took it out, over and over, as if the body could learn only in this way, only by repetition, over and over and over until I didn't know which was him, which was me, and I felt liquid, as if I might slip out of myself, and again I was afraid. I put my hands on his shoulders, pulled him up toward me, touched his face. I wanted him to open his eyes and look at me, to prove that it was him and that he knew it was me, and he did. "Jesse," he said. Then he pushed himself inside me in one motion, filling me up, taking my breath.

I never got tired of making love to him, even after all those months—how long had it been? Four, five?—and I wondered if the feeling would ever wear off, whether he would look at me one day without desire, maybe even with disgust.

"Do you think you'll ever get sick of me?" I asked.

"Sick of you? Never," he said, pulling me closer, moving his hand down my belly, resting it there.

"I love you, you know," I said very quietly, not looking at him.

"I know," he said. "Scary, isn't it."

"Yes. You've got that right."

When the light was gone from the room, he got up, put on his white terry-cloth robe, and knotted the tie at his waist.

"Hungry?"

"Starving."

"Bacon and eggs all right?"

"Fine," I said, but I felt so heavy I couldn't keep my eyes open.

"Jesse, Jesse." He was shaking me.

"I must have fallen asleep." I was drenched in sweat; my hands were slick with it.

"You were talking a blue streak." He put his palm on my right cheek, rubbed his thumb over my lips, a gesture both sexual and consoling. "Bad dream?"

"The usual." It's a dream I've had all my life, or as far back as I can remember.

We ate the eggs and bacon in silence. It was a good silence, of two people grown comfortable with each other, war buddies, childhood friends.

When we were finished eating, he took my plate, stacked it on his, and set them both on the floor beside the bed.

"Tell me about the dream," he said, touching my wrist, keeping his fingers and thumb there, as if taking my pulse.

"Other people's dreams are boring."

"Tell me."

"Okay. Remember you asked for it." I looked at him and he nodded. I cleared my throat, swallowed hard, began.

"In the dream I dream of my father. He is floating above my desk. It's a desk I used to have, a large desk, with drawers on both sides, made of oak. In the dream he is floating above my desk. His face. Just his face." I used my hands to demonstrate. "This smiling countenance. You know, the way God is drawn in cartoons, cloud-like, benign."

"Mm-hmm."

"There is a mathematical problem I must solve. If I can't find the solution in time, my father will die. I'm not sure how I know this—no one tells me this in the dream—but I know, the way you know . . . when someone loves you."

I looked at him and he smiled.

"I work feverishly, against some imagined clock, because I don't even know how much time I've got. It could be minutes, hours, months. But it doesn't matter anyway, I can't get it right, no matter how many times I begin again, wadding up sheets and sheets of white paper, trembling, the ink of the pen coming off on my hands. That's the way it ends, the ending is always the same—the ink of the pen coming off on my hands, and I look at it in horror, as if it were blood." I smiled. "Well, what do you make of it, Herr Doktor Freud?"

He held me then and he didn't say anything, not a word. And for the first time in my life I thought: I could stay here forever.

Season of Grief

"When a person has only one thing in the world—namely, a certain talent—what is he to do when he begins to lose that talent?"

My father sat staring still in the square oak chair with the thin slats on three sides like a baby's crib and the red leather cushions with the large covered buttons that pinch, his chicken-pale legs sticking out from the blue flannel robe, fallen open. Burnt at the stake of some longing I can't recall, I had come to him, hoping that he would smile at me, smooth my hair with his large blue-veined hands, whisper, "Jesse, such a thing to make a giant cry," some half-forgotten line from a fairy tale he had given a new meaning. Instead, he pulled the hems of his robe together between his knees, a pigeon-toed school-girl, put his head back against the stiff cushion, closed his eyes.

In the moment of that slow question he was transformed, gone from father-storyteller-god to an ordinary old man in a frayed robe. I was pierced by his frailty, indignant that he could turn pitiful, pale, and would no longer help me in my war on the truth-telling world that made me small.

In a cracked voice I said, "Daddy, I don't *know.*"

The pigs started to die at the end of April, drowning facedown in their own muck. Lucky and I carried the smallest and most slippery to the barn, made a bed of hay in the loft for their pink swollen bodies, fed them whey from a bottle as if they were human babies.

I have little sympathy, as I have said, for these animals that seem to me unclean, the embodiment of everything ignoble. But death changes the essence of a thing.

The sound of their pain was terrible; it filled my dreams for weeks. And the land was littered with pigs, fallen in different postures of defeat, but always this—facedown, dead eyes staring into the mud.

"What good is a pig farmer without any pigs?" When the news came in from the vet—trichinosis, fatal—Lucky sat up late drinking and reading Yeats, "To a Friend Whose Work Has Come to Nothing," asking himself this and other hard questions.

He spent every night in the barn, as if sympathy or even love could keep them breathing, then brought the last live one to the house and laid it in our bed, gave it a name.

"Either that pig goes or I do," I said.

By the end of the week, Prometheus was dead.

"They can kill you but they can't eat you," Lucky said over the grave he dug at the back of the barn and covered with dandelions. To himself or to the pig, I don't know. I put my hand on his arm and he didn't move it away, but neither did he acknowledge any comfort from it, and I didn't know what to say.

The real estate assessor came that afternoon, a tall thin man in a green three-piece polyester suit, with a face like a ferret.

Lucky showed him around the house first, but he didn't take note of the refinished wooden floors, a light shade of oak, or the newly laid linoleum, dark blue, in the kitchen, or the walls and high ceilings, just-painted white. Outside, the assessor scraped the foundation with a knife, made a face like sucking lemons, then wrote something down on his clipboard.

"It's like watching your own postmortem," Lucky said.

"Yessirree," the assessor cheerfully agreed.

I went back into the house while he showed the assessor the land, because I didn't want to see Lucky's face when he looked at the creek, the hills, the perfect rows of corn through the assessor's eyes.

"Do you want to know the secret to success?" Lucky asked when he came back in, as I heard the gravel grind under the wheels of the hearse. "I'll tell you." He put his hand at the back of my neck, pulled my face toward his face, nose to nose. "Buy high, sell low." Then he laughed, a sound like vomiting, and I wanted to give him something but I didn't know what.

"What are you going to do?" I asked this question over and over, not knowing myself, wondering what the sale of the farm meant for us, if we would continue together, what would become of us.

"Tell me a story," he said, touching me in circles, his fingers like an argument with no conclusion or a question repeating.

"Which one do you want to hear?"

"The one about your father."

"The true one or the lie?"

"The one with the happy ending," he said, making a circle with his thumb and forefinger around my wrist.

I began.

"That evening in August the world went dark right after supper and the lightning storm banged the door against the house with such force that I whimpered and hung at my father's knees."

"Poor baby."

"That was the first time he told me the story about the giant who cried at the rain."

"Let's hear it."

"Well, there's this giant, see. And this giant is the most powerful man in a kingdom of pygmies. But he has a small problem: when the rain falls, he shrinks. Unfortunately for the giant this kingdom has a season of rain that lasts nine months of the year. Like Portland, Oregon."

"I've been there."

"His greatest fear is shrinking to the size of the pygmies, whose legs are so short that it takes them all day just to walk to work and back."

"I know the feeling."

"So the giant spends his days inside the house, his giant nose pressed against a giant windowpane. It's rain season and he is afraid. And also slightly jealous, watching the pygmies walking about, free, catching raindrops on their tiny tongues, building castles in the mud. Looking out at the pygmies he begins to cry. Giant tears roll down his giant face."

"And?"

"He shrinks, of course, poor bastard. Until he's so small he can't even see out the window."

"The moral?" Lucky asked.

"Damned if you do, damned if you don't."

He laughed. "That's not the moral," he said. "That's not what you told me the last time."

"I've revised it slightly. For the occasion."

"I see. Please continue."

"Well, my father told me this story, or something close to it, then he took off my shoes and socks, his own as well, took my hand, and led me out into the early night, where he taught me to shake my fist at the rain."

"Show me how."

"Like this," I said, and we lay there on the bed, assaulting the air.

"My mother was inside washing dishes and he went in to get her but she wouldn't come out."

"Why not?"

"I don't know. Maybe she thought washing dishes was more important. Maybe she was afraid herself."

He ran a thumbnail up the inside of my thigh. "What then?"

"He put on Richard Strauss—maybe to spite her, maybe for the drama of it—and turned it up so loud I thought we'd all be stone deaf or stupid, then came back out. With Strauss playing, the thunder and lightning, branches cracking overhead, the rain—I thought that this must be what heaven is like, or hell, the best light show on earth, and I felt such a terrible joy that I forgot my fear and shook my fist at the sky. Harder! he yelled, then to the storm, Frig on!"

"Is that part of the story?" he asked, smiling down at me.

"I see him now, a giant with scrawny arms in a soaked T-shirt, his eyes lit up like a video game."

"And?"

"He was struck by lightning. But he lived."

"Lucky," Lucky said and smiled.

"Do you want to know the moral?" I asked, and he nodded. I made my voice shake like Katharine Hepburn's in *On Golden Pond:* "Every fist the world has loses against those eyes."

"Say it straight," he said.

These hands.

It's odd to be living in a house that's already sold; it's what the terminally ill must feel, having received the final notice but unable to believe in their absolute dispossession. Everyday life takes on the disconnected brilliance of a memory—the sun striking three mason jars on a counter, the shadow of a hand on a thigh in the last half moon, pale bare feet on dark blue linoleum. Mourning precedes the loss and doubles it, making every gesture significant, every object a warning: this is what you have lost, will go on losing.

At the end of the gravel road I stand staring at the names on the mailbox—Redbord in faded flat black, Walker in high-gloss white—as a moviegoer will pointlessly watch the closing credits, names of hairdressers, stuntmen, body doubles, unwilling yet to leave the comfort of the dark, the captured light. I have made this place my own and do not want to go.

But already there are cardboard boxes where we stood, marked *bedroom, living room, kitchen, bath.* We are deserting the house, dismantling ourselves, bone by bone. Sixty days seems too long to wait—it will be summer then, a new season to lose. Wouldn't it be better to burn it down? I think, and understand that self-destruction is the last positive act of the powerless.

Earl and Kathleen invited us out to dinner to try to cheer Lucky up—Chez Fred's, a new French place with pretensions.

"Too many forks, let's go," Lucky said as soon as we sat down.

I laughed too loud and everyone turned to stare.

"Whatsamatter, haven't you folks ever heard anyone laugh before?" he asked in his dumb pig farmer voice.

The waiter, dressed in funeral black, leaned toward us, an attitude slightly superior to the wine, as it turned out. "May I bring you. A cocktail. Before dinner?" he asked, nostrils flaring.

"I'd blow a goat for a bottle of beer," Lucky said, and the waiter jerked back so hard I thought he'd broken his neck. He never asked again without flinching if he could get us anything.

We didn't talk much during dinner, except for Kathleen, who kept saying, "I'm sorry. I'm *so* sorry," shredding her napkin until it looked like snow on her steak Béarnaise.

"Tant piss," Lucky said, to soothe her.

I put my hand on his arm, wanting to say something, wanting him to say something to me. He looked at me hopefully for a moment, but then went back to eating.

The rest of the time there was only the click of silverware against the plates, overheard conversations. Somber, that's what it was. As if someone had died, and I wondered if it was us.

"I've got it," Earl said when the check came, probably the only time in his life Earl has used those words in that connection.

After dinner we went over to the Stoneleigh P with the intention of drinking ourselves into a better mood.

"I thought I'd never sell that farm," Lucky said at the end of the third round of silence.

"What are you going to do now?" Earl asked.

Lucky looked at me. "I don't know. Maybe I could interest my former employer in a dead pig book. What do you think?"

I sat there studying my fingernails, not knowing the proper response to this. What do you say to somebody who's just put his life on the market? And I didn't know if he wanted to stay with me, a question I'd been thinking a lot about but was too proud to ask.

"Oh hell, forget it," Lucky said. Then his face brightened. "There's something I want to show you," he said, turning our attention to the Lone Tree beer sign behind the bar. "Right after the second tree from the corner. See it?"

The three of us crowded around the bar and stared at where he was pointing, but either you had to know exactly where to look in the moving water or we were already too drunk, or both. All I could see was a man in a canoe and some trees, the neon water so blue it made my head hurt.

"The way I heard it," Lucky said, "the artist had contracted with this beer company for a certain amount of cash for this very sign." Here he gestured grandly, knocking over somebody's beer bottle. "Pardon me," he said. "But it must've been a bad year for the company, or maybe they weren't satisfied with the quality of his work. Whatever the reason was, they refused to pay this man what they had promised when he was done. So, to show his own dissatisfaction, he wrote *fuck* in the water in the Lone Tree beer sign."

Just then I saw Sally Lawson rubbing her black stockings up and down Mike Maniaci's Levi's under the table in the corner. I don't know how her husband could see what was happening under that table but he did. He slapped Sally so hard I'm sure her ears rang for a week. She got up—with some dignity, I thought, under the circumstances—and walked out of the bar. Nobody laid a hand on Jerry Lawson.

"I think somebody should teach Jerry Lawson some respect for women," I said.

"I'd never hit a woman," Earl said.

Kathleen kissed him. "I know you wouldn't, honey," she said.

"I just don't think a man should strike a woman," Earl said, sitting up a little straighter in his seat, and all of us nodded except Lucky. He was sucking on his beer looking thoughtful, like he does a lot of the time, and I wondered if he was even listening.

"I hit a woman once," he said slowly, "in a bar in Pittsburgh."

"What a man," I said.

"She was somebody I used to meet for a drink sometimes, after Annie and I split up. Nobody special, but she could be good company," he said, taking a straw from my glass and chewing it. "She and Annie had been friends, and she kept saying what a shame it was we'd split. I said yes, it was that—a shame—but I couldn't see any way around it after some of the things we'd said. No taking some things back, I said."

I wanted to know what ugly things were said, and by whom, but I was waiting for what seemed the more important point: why he'd hit her. What I really wanted to know, though, was where, on the continuum from good company to wife, I stood.

"Then this *woman*"—he sort of spit this word, like it was something obscene—"says, Yeah, Annie was a real slut. I could tell you some stories about Annie. I said I didn't want to hear her stories and I didn't appreciate her calling my wife a slut."

I didn't appreciate the passion he was bringing to Annie's defense, but I was glad to be learning something about his past without having to beg for once, so I shut up and listened.

"Well," Lucky continued, "she seemed to know she'd found a fresh wound in the dark, and she starts saying slut, slut, slut, in this soft and vicious voice. Slut, slut, slut," he repeated, beginning to choke his beer bottle. He sat there quiet for a moment, as if he were remembering something else, a memory that left me out. "Well, I listened to this for a while, thinking of all Annie and I had been to each other, and how this woman's meanness mattered little in the larger world, and of that thing my mother used to say about sticks and stones, but none of it did any good. Slut, slut, slut," he said, his voice rising in the smoky darkness.

Some guy at the bar, across from us, looked down at me from his barstool and shook his head in what I could only take to be pity, and I wished Lucky would quit saying *slut* and get to the point.

"Well, she said it one time too many and I slapped her. She fell off the barstool and three heroes shoved me up against the bar and said, That's no way to treat a lady, and I said, That's why I slapped her, and they looked at me like I was drunk or stupid, then did to me what they'd been wanting to do to somebody all night."

"Did you regret it?" I asked.

"Yes," he said. "I did. But I'd do it again."

"Can you regret something you've done and still say you would do it again?"

I was trying to figure this out when Earl said, from several inches above his hair, "If there's nothing you wouldn't do, you're just an animal in blue jeans." Looking at Lucky.

"These are not *just* blue jeans, Earl," Kathleen said—at which point Earl turned his close-set eyes on her—and you could see by her flinch that she knew it was a mistake before the words had come into full meaning.

"Listen to this," I said, hoping to rescue Kathleen from the beady-eyed Earl. "Suppose you're standing on the shore alone and your wife is out swimming in the ocean."

"Your wife," Kathleen said, but Earl was looking at me.

"She starts to flounder. Maybe a storm has come up all of a sudden, maybe she's too far out, or maybe she just can't swim. It doesn't matter. What matters is that at this very moment, two children, strangers to yourself, strangers swimming peacefully only moments before, start to gulp and yell help as well. You can't save them all. What do you do?"

"You save your wife," Lucky said.

"But why should two strangers die just because this woman happens to be your wife? Imagine you are one of those strangers. How would you feel about *that?*"

"Sorry as hell," Lucky said. "But I'd still save my wife."

"You can't be *both* the man on the shore and one of the strangers," I said with some exasperation. "That doesn't make any sense."

"I don't care if it makes any sense. People are more important," Lucky said, though the look of disgust he gave me suggested an exception.

"I'd save the children," Earl said. "Two lives are worth more than one."

"But she's your *wife,*" Kathleen said, looking at Earl with her own eyes.

"I can't help it," Earl said. "That's the way I feel."

"Or don't," Lucky said.

Emmylou Harris was singing "Ashes by Now" on the jukebox, and Kathleen began to hum softly along with the music. Earl was sitting there stuffed in his shirt, oblivious, and Lucky was, between his two moods of brooding and morose, clearly favoring morose. I decided to let it drop, and we all ordered another drink.

Earl got up to go to the bathroom and came back looking like a man with a purpose. "What wouldn't *you* do?" he said to Kathleen after the waitress had come with our drinks and cleared the debris from the table.

Kathleen looked dubious, like a kid who's been slapped too many times in the supermarket and now won't even get out of the car.

"We'd like to hear, Kathleen," I said and gave her an encouraging look. This was for Lucky's benefit. He thinks I'm too hard on Kathleen most of the time and I wanted him to know that I was trying. He rubbed my knuckle with his thumb to let me know he knew, and I felt almost peaceful.

"*Well,* Kathleen?" Earl said, after a few minutes of napkin-shredding silence.

Kathleen chewed on her lip and moved her eyes like a kid in the last heat of a spelling contest. "I—" She started to say something but stopped. "I—" You could see her eyes going from side to side, fearful, considering. "I would never intentionally hurt anyone," she said finally.

Earl looked disappointed, and Lucky did that thing again with his thumb.

"That's a very nice sentiment, Kathleen," I said, "but can you exist in the world without hurting anyone?"

For a moment there was silence and Lucky drew his hand back.

"I'd never hurt an innocent *child,*" Earl said, trying to recapture the spirit of his recent triumph.

"As the man said, Never attempt to teach a pig to sing. It wastes your time and annoys the pig," Lucky said, staring off at the Lone Tree beer sign.

I didn't know whether this was directed at Earl or at me, but I decided to let it pass, in the interest of harmony and in light of his recent loss. Earl was another story. I couldn't stand the way the smugness still sat on his lips.

"Consider the following case," I said. "Suppose some Argentinean guerrillas have poisoned the water supply in some large American city. New York, Chicago, L.A., maybe, but you don't know which. And the only one who knows is Jose, the Argentineans' main man, and he isn't talking. Not until their demands are met anyway."

"And what. Are their demands," Earl asked. You could say he looked sceptical, but his eyes are so close together it's hard to tell.

"It doesn't matter. Use your imagination. Say it's something of crucial importance to national security. Say anything you like. If their demands aren't met by midnight, a hundred thousand American people, maybe more, will die in agony before breakfast."

"I think I could make him talk," Lucky said quietly.

"This is my story," I said, "and in my story the only way to make Jose talk is to torture Jose junior. What do you do?"

"What do *you* do?" Earl asked. "You're real long on the questions and real short on the answers."

"Yeah," Lucky said. "Your story. *Your* story. That's the point, isn't it?"

I looked at him hard. I'd tried to understand the things he'd told me, hadn't I? Tried to imagine what it was like to be him, flinched

125

when he hurt, kissed it to make it better. Hadn't I? *Your* story. The son of a bitch! I felt tears starting and blinked them back.

"What would you do *if* this and this and this," Lucky continued. "Well, my answer is life isn't like that. You don't *get* to make up all the rules. It's the big boys down at the bank or the FHA that decide who lives and dies. And they play hardball, not some cheap little mind game."

"Touché," Earl said.

"I don't have to take this shit," I said and lit a cigarette. "But just for the record, I wouldn't torture little Jose. I'd get my brother to do it."

"That's right," Lucky said. "Let somebody else do the dirty work. Just so you keep your lily-white hands clean."

This sounded like a reference to more than how to break Jose, and it pissed me off. I'd worked my ass off trying to save those disgusting pigs, I'd fed them like babies, ignoring the smell, held Lucky's hand when he buried the one who'd taken over my side of the bed, and this was the thanks I got for it. *There's* a moral for you, I thought, and pretty goddamn easy to read. The more I thought about it, the madder I got, and when I had worked myself up into a frenzy of self-righteous rage, I flung my left arm into Lucky's stomach.

He grabbed my wrist and held it, looking at me like I had dirt or worse under my fingernails, which I probably did, thanks to him. *"I'll* tell you what you'd do," he said. "You'd watch the world burn while you told your fucking fairy tales. I know. I've seen it. And if you want to know the truth I've had a bellyful of it."

"Let go of my arm!" I said, yanking it back. I yanked again. When that failed, I began prying his fingers off.

He held my arm a moment longer, just looking at it, as if trying to decide what to do with a sick squirrel he'd caught.

"Big. Man," I said.

He let go and I banged my elbow hard on the table. Then he half rose in his seat, jarring the table and spilling my drink in my lap.

"Jesus Christ," I said, sopping it up as well as I could with the wet napkins.

"Get out of my way," he said, too quietly to dismiss as a polite request. He was still half risen in the corner, looking down at me.

"Come on, you guys," Kathleen said.

"Yeah," Earl said. "Lighten up."

But I didn't feel light, I felt hurt and mean, and I threw my wet napkins at him.

"Get out of my way," he repeated, picking the soggy pieces of paper from his face and flinging them down.

"What are you going to do if I don't? *Hit* me?"

"I'm asking you to get out of my way," he said slowly.

"This has gone quite far enough," Earl said, reaching over and yanking on the front of Lucky's shirt, trying to get him to sit down.

He didn't budge.

"Yes," Kathleen said. "Let's talk about something else."

Lucky slammed his fist on the table, breaking Earl's grip on his shirt, making the glasses jump and strangers stare. "The trouble with *you,*" he said, "is that you have never thought you were moral scum."

I knew he was talking to me.

"My God," he said, "what things have we done in the name of the things we would never do."

"Thinking you're moral scum," I said, in a shrill and rising voice, "is no proof of emotional honesty. And anyway, rolling in the muck is not the *best* way of getting clean. As a former pig farmer of *all* people *should know*!"

He looked at me then like I had just gone out of existence and stood all the way up, pinning Earl and Kathleen against the wall with the table. Glasses slid toward the edge, hovered, went over. The ashtray emptied itself in Kathleen's lap.

"Get. Out. Of. My. Way."

I wanted to say, Don't go. I wanted to say that he was wrong, that I had done some things I regretted, that I couldn't make right. I wanted to say that I had seen the morning when my whole world was shamed, when I was nothing but a whimper in a dark place. I wanted to bring him my humiliations like a gift. But I just sat there looking superior.

"Get out of my way, Jesse." He said it quietly but I could see the disgust in his mean and narrow eyes. I don't think I'd ever seen that look on anyone's face. The force with which he wanted to get away from me was frightening.

I took my hand off his arm. "Fuck," I said. "If that's the way you feel, just get the hell *out*!" Then I added, almost as an afterthought, looking up at him, "Maybe it's not too late. Maybe your *slut wife* will take you back."

His eyes deserted his face and I watched as his hand, open palmed, made a slow-motion arc toward me.

Whack.

I fell off the bench onto the floor, clutching my face. I started to wail, scared more by what could have happened than by what did.

Lucky stepped over me like he was stepping over pig shit and walked toward the door. Kathleen helped me up, just in time to see him go through it.

"Bastard!" I yelled. "Son of a *bitch*!"

Merle Haggard was singing "I Think I'll Just Stay Here and Drink" on the jukebox—which, after Lucky left, I did. When the song was over, Earl said it was getting late, and he and Kathleen got up to go. Kathleen touched my shoulder before she left, though I don't know what she meant by it.

I sat there drinking and wondering what I was supposed to do then. After a few more Scotch and waters and a trip to the restroom to see the damage that was done—a slight red welt of a handprint on the left side of my face—I asked the bartender if I could look at the Lone Tree sign up close, behind the bar. He said all right, since most everyone was gone by that hour.

I stared at that sign for a long time, trying to spot it. I watched the water and the trees and the man in the canoe go by several times. I looked into that harsh blue light until my eyes ached and I felt slightly nauseous. Then I saw it.

"Fuck," I said, like a prayer. But saying it didn't make me feel any better. I went back to the table. I sat there meditating on my melting ice cubes, life and death. I wondered where Lucky was, if he'd gone back to the farm or what. I supposed I'd have to walk home alone in the dark. Seven miles. Might as well get going, I thought, but I didn't have the heart to get up. I didn't feel proud or outraged any longer, I just felt lonely. I kept looking at the door, hoping Lucky would come back. There was something I wanted to tell him.

He didn't come back into the Stoneleigh P that night. I waited until the bar closed and he still didn't show.

I remember walking through the empty streets. I walked slowly, limping to myself. Past an old Victorian with one high light in the window. Past Mulligan's Feed Store, where rats the size of woodchucks scurried in and out among the broken sacks of grain. Past A-OK Used Cars, strung with red, white, and blue plastic pennants, where the car on display—a rusted-out brown MGB—looked like it had been mistakenly saved from the car-crushing machine, *Make an Offer* written in soap on the windshield. Past a string of derelict houses, their porches rolling like waves. Past a sign that read: *Dubuque. City of Five Seasons.* The fifth, I wondered. What is it? I walked the seven miles out to the farm, but there was no sign of Lucky's truck and the place was locked up tight. I felt like I'd been locked out of my own house, I'd spent so much time in it.

Out of perversity or a desire for further punishment, I stayed. It was a sleepless night in the loft, with shadows of pigs for company. All through the night, with the sticks of hay assaulting my skin, I rehearsed what I would say if he was still listening. "Maybe I was wrong. Maybe I have spent my life writing *fuck* in the water when I should have been writing something else."

But by dawn the fragile thought had died of exhaustion and self-righteousness had a renaissance. "The man *struck* you!" I said aloud, my words small and hollow in the empty barn. "In the *face!*" I have always had a clear sense of the unforgivable, at least with respect to the behavior of others, and it seemed clear to me then that Lucky had crossed some line there was no redrawing.

I put on my boots, stood unsteadily on the scattered hay in the loft, dusted myself off, pulled my fingers through my hair, then backed down the ladder I had built only months before. I had a slight headache from too much Scotch or being slapped upside the head, I wasn't sure which, but I walked purposefully out of the barn. The sun was coming up, glinting off the rain gutters. I looked at the house, the fields, looked at them hard, tried to commit them to memory, tried to see what the sum of it came to.

I saw a slit of light at the edge of the kitchen window. I walked over, put my fingertips under it, lifted it up, smiled to myself, as if the open window were proof of my cleverness, crawled in, stuck one foot in the sink, then the other, jumped down, slipped on the linoleum floor, and fell flat on my ass. I lay there for a few minutes, staring up at the white ceiling, seeing a place I'd missed in painting, a moon-shaped arc of off-white in the corner.

It's an odd feeling—breaking into what you have heretofore believed to be your own house. I picked myself up, opened the drawer beside the sink, took out ten twenty-dollar bills, folded them over, and stuffed them into my pocket. I figured I'd earned it. More.

I looked around the kitchen, at the round oak table, an empty white coffee mug on it, as if someone had just finished. "Sayonara, sweetie," I said with what bravado I could manage. But I felt a pain start at the back of my neck, begin to spread through my arms, my legs. "Son of a *bitch*!" I said, as loud as I could, to make it stop. Then I climbed back out the window, as if to use the front door would be too much of a concession, though I didn't know to what.

I took off his boots, one at a time, hopping to keep my balance, and threw them against the side of the house. The boots landed with a nice satisfying *thunk,* the toes pointing in opposite directions, as if someone, undecided and hoping for guidance, had thrown them like dice. I studied the boots, trying to decide whether to take this as an omen, a sign. But then I touched my hand to my face. "Lucky," I said and snorted. "Lucky I'm still *alive*!"

I looked down at my stockinged feet with something like pride. I was going the way I'd come, without any shoes. "Travel light," I said, as if someone had stuck a microphone in my face and asked me to name the one indispensable rule for living.

An image of Lucky standing in the front doorway with a toothpick in his mouth, the fingers of one hand in a front pocket, imposed itself on my mind. *You won't get very far in this snow dressed like that.* I pushed it away. No snow now. May. What day was it? The sixteenth? Seventeenth?

Then another image came—him standing in the doorway of the bathroom, me still wet from the shower. *I'm sorry. I didn't know . . .* I started to cry, but I wasn't stupid enough any longer to think my imagining meant anything except that I was good at imagining what would make me cry.

I headed toward town, staying on the edge of the blacktop so I'd have something flat to walk on. About a mile gone with my socks falling down and my feet starting to hurt, it came to me—the Jaguar in the barn: I could take it. Something to remember him by. Would he call the police, have me arrested? Come after me himself? Even while I was asking these questions I was turning around, heading back toward the house, grinning as I began to run. I knew where the key was hidden—in a magnetized metal box under the hood—and while I ran I imagined opening it up, sliding the key out of the metal box, snapping the hood shut, turning the key in the lock, opening the door, slipping in behind the wheel of the car, liking the feel of the red leather seats. For a moment I was my father, and I heard the thrilling words over the loudspeaker, "Gentlemen, start your engines," the cheering of the crowd in the stands, and the collective roar as the engines came to life, the vibration of the air itself, a buzzing inside my chest, in my hands, and then the falling of the flag. I saw myself backing out through the double doors of the barn, closing them behind me. I pulled onto the road, watched the farm grow small in the rearview mirror, hit forty, fifty, sixty, seventy, keeping the shiny silver hood ornament lined up with the edge of the road like a gun sight. I reached down and turned the knob on the radio. Nothing except static. I switched it off, then I began to sing, at the top of my lungs—"Bird on the Wire," "Ramblin' Fever," "Willin'," "Cry Like a Rainstorm," "Adios," "Turn the Page"—all the leaving-town songs I knew. When Lucky came back from wherever his anger or pride had taken him, I would be halfway across the next state, thinking of this place only in the past tense, long gone.

On the Road Again

"I never knew the road from which the whole earth didn't call away, with wild birds rounding the hill crowns, haling out of the heart an old dismay, or the shore somewhere pounding its slow code, or low-lighted towns seeming to tell me, stay . . ." I speak in a low and melancholy voice. "Lands I have never seen and shall not see, loves I will not forget, all I have missed, or slighted, or foregone . . . call to me now. And weaken me. And yet I would not walk a road without a scene. I listen going on, the richer for regret."

I have moved on from leaving-town songs to leaving-town poems when the hood of the Jag flies up in my face, covering the windshield, making it impossible to see in front of me. I slam on the brakes and look in my rearview mirror just in time to see a Bekins van bearing down on me, blowing his horn. I feel first terror, then disbelief, then resignation, and I duck down my head until I'm eye-level with the top of the steering wheel, peer through the crack of light between the edge of the hood and the body of the car, and I can see just enough to get off to the side of the highway without doing any more damage, either to myself or to the car.

"Goddamn *son* of a bitch!" I turn off the key, roll down the window for some air, and sit there, shaking. Even when you know you're safe, it takes your body a while to believe it.

"You okay?" the man asks, sticking his head inside the window. He is big—six-three, six-four—blond, broken-nosed. Not over twenty-one.

"I don't believe this," I say. "This is too bad to be true."

He walks around to the front of the car and looks it over. I can see him shaking his head, impartially disgusted. Then there is the scrape of metal on metal, a crunching sound, as he bends the hood back down, presses on it until I hear the click of the hood latch. The hood is no longer smooth; it looks like somebody tried to open it with a can opener.

"That oughta get you to the next gas station or a body shop where you can get it fixed," he says. "Somebody didn't shut the hood all the way. That's the only thing I can figure."

Somebody. Me.

"What a shame. It's a beautiful car."

"It was."

"You sure you're okay?"

"Physically," I say. "Morally, I could use a drink."

"I'm really sorry," he says, smiling like you do at the stupid, shaking his head with goodwill. He taps the flat of his hand on the roof of the car, says, "Good luck," and walks off toward his truck, climbs up into it, pulls back onto the highway, blowing his horn in farewell.

"Now what?" I say, but I know nobody is listening. I haven't even made it out of Iowa.

It reminds me of the first time I ran away from home—with my brother, David. He was nine and I was seven. I don't remember the cause of our outrage, why we thought we could no longer stay with such people in such an intolerable place. But I do remember that I was barefoot and we were walking on gravel—the gravel road that leads from our house to the highway—and my brother was lamenting how I slowed him down, how he was tired of my whining about my feet, how he shouldn't have brought me along to start with. I was beginning to have second thoughts myself. We hadn't even made it to the cattle guard before we saw a cloud of dust moving toward us: our father in the pickup, doing sixty on the rutted gravel road. When he caught up with us at the mailbox, he said, "Get in," and we did, neither defiant nor apologetic, but as if we had just been out for a walk and were glad for the lift home.

I decide to stop at the next town, whatever it is, and call Lucky, ask him to come and get me; no, beg. But the more I think about it the less I can imagine what I might say. "Hi, this is Jesse. Your pretty white Jaguar is wrecked but I'm all right." That might work at sixteen with your mother's station wagon, but with him I don't have that kind of liability insurance.

So I hit the next town—Tennyson—stop for gas, and keep going.

By the side of the road every so often are curved guardrails coming up out of the ground, then going back in, something I've never seen in all my years of moving around. It makes the highway seem like a huge roller coaster, and I think of the Giant Dipper at the boardwalk at Santa Cruz. We always rode in the front car, my father and I, with our arms above our heads, to prove we weren't afraid.

To the left I see a dead animal, a slaughtered dog. To the right, a man riding a John Deere tractor is cutting his grass, decapitating all the dandelions, leaving only the field of green.

I come to a fork in the road and I can't decide what to do, whether to go east on 121 or keep going north, then I see a sign that reads:

DISCOVER LANCASTER
Take Route 61

so I do.

I drive for a while in silence. The only sound in the world is my stomach growling.

I stop for lunch at a little place called the Blue Light Café. The waitress looks like every waitress, and the oilcloth-covered table is so greasy my forearms stick to it. I order the Blue Light Special for $2.95—a hot roast beef sandwich—thinking that will be hard to ruin, but the food is generic, too, bland, tasteless, all brown except for the forlorn sprig of parsley drowning in the gravy. I leave the waitress a two-dollar tip because I feel sorrier for her than for myself. There's no one else in the place and it's nowhere near quitting time.

I get back into the car with no detailed plan in mind, thinking I'll just keep driving until something comes to me. I hum a little to myself but my heart isn't in it.

It's close to dark and the tank is near empty when the red ENGINE light comes on, then goes off, like a blinking bloodshot eye. With my genius for diagnosis, I suppose this means the engine is overheated. I pull off to the side of the highway and wait for the engine to cool down. I'm no longer singing any songs or reciting any poetry. I am disgusted with myself and tired, tired way deep down. I feel as if I have just left the only home I will ever have, left it of my own accord, and there's no way back. I start to cry and bite my knuckles to make it stop. *Sissygirl.* I wipe my eyes with the back of my hand and turn on the ignition, but it won't start. I try again. This time the engine doesn't even turn over. Dead. My luck is holding.

I get out of the car, slam the door shut, and curse, but I can't think of any words bad enough to fit the occasion. I walk on in the direction in which I have been traveling, not for any certain purpose but only because it's one way or the other and if you're walking alone it doesn't much matter which; like the generic waitress, every road is the same.

It is still light, though just barely, and I study the signs as I pass for some clue as to what I should do next. On the right side of the road, I see a sign with blue and red balloons:

NEED A LIFT?

CALL ON JESUS

On the other side of the road, less than fifty yards farther on:

REBUILT ENGINES

DON'S TRANSMISSIONS

I decide I'll take my chances with Don.

But Don doesn't answer when I knock on the door of his garage, three miles down the road, and so I keep walking, for lack of an attractive alternative, even after dark.

I come to a little dive a couple of miles farther on, what looks like a house trailer turned into a bar, with only a neon Lone Tree beer sign for a name. I go inside to get some change from the bartender and make a telephone call from the phone on the wall near the door. There are, I notice while the telephone is ringing, only two backs at the bar.

"Hello?"

"Hi. This is Jesse, your errant sister."

"Are you all right?" she asks right away.

"I've been better," I say. "But if you've got everything you want, you're not asking for enough."

She laughs. "Where are you calling from?"

"I don't know. Somewhere north of Iowa, I think."

"I could come and get you. It can't be more than a two-day drive from here." She lives in Missoula, Montana.

"Ellie," I say, my voice going soft.

"What, Baby?"

There is a click and the sound of coins falling in a far place.

"I've got to go find some more change. I'll call you right back."

"No. Let me call you back."

"Okay." I give her the number, then wait, looking out at the night, remembering a time long ago.

At the limit of our land was an oak tree with two long low-lying branches, like arms, that we were forbidden to ride. Our mother said the tree looked strong but was rotten inside and would not hold us.

Ellen did it anyway. Mama would make her cut her own switch when she caught her. But because she didn't have the heart to beat her every day, she finally gave up and said, "If you fall out of that tree and break your leg, don't come running to me."

I watched Ellen from our bedroom window one night, watched her take off her robe and slippers in the moonlight—midnight stripper—and climb on in her frayed white flannel nightgown. I lay awake until she came in, tiptoeing across the room to her bed, pulling the comforter up under her chin, the way Mama did when she tucked me in, staring straight up at the ceiling.

"Ellen?" I whispered.

"What, Baby?"

"Are you all right?"

"I was almost flying, Jesse. I went so high I thought maybe my heart would give out. Feel it," she said, and I got up and went over to put my hand on her chest. It felt like the old washer on SPIN.

But the day I am thinking about is different. I was five or six at the time, not yet in school. That would make Ellen twelve or thirteen. In the afternoons I would wait for her to come home. Standing at the end of our driveway where the gravel road begins that leads to the highway, I would watch her grow larger and larger in the long afternoon, and a feeling would take hold in my stomach. *Ellen's home.* She'd smooth my hair and call me Baby, or punch me in the arm and say, "Hi, kid," depending on her mood. That day she cut out across the salt-grass hills without changing her good yellow school dress, headed straight for the tree, and I knew something bad must've happened.

I followed her and watched her climb on, push off with her feet. She was repeating something over and over that I couldn't hear. When she was as high as I'd ever seen her go, she stretched out her long legs and, on the upswing, pushed again with the tips of her toes, went higher still. "Ellen!" I screamed, but she didn't answer. When she let go with her hands, I ran to get Mama, my heart beating as hard as Ellen's had that night.

I was maybe twenty feet gone when I heard the branch crack. I looked back and saw Ellen falling. By the time I got to her, she lay in a twisted yellow lump, face down, unholy quiet. At first I thought she was dead. Then she rolled over and sat up, began picking pebbles and twigs out of knees that looked like raw hamburger. In a minute she gave that up. She held her knees and rocked. Her dress was ripped at the shoulder and in the front. There was blood all over it.

"He *hurt* me, Jesse," she said, and then she let out this sound. Not crying but something past crying. It made me afraid to ask who it was or what he had done.

I walked back with her across the field to the house, holding her elbow, the only gesture of caring I could manage at my height.

The telephone is ringing.

"It's me again," Ellen says. "What are you doing in Iowa?"

"I'm making friends with a rebuilt engine."

"If it's money . . ."

"No." I don't like taking money from people related to me by force.

"Is there anything you need?"

"Some shoes. A new Jaguar."

She laughs, thinks I'm kidding.

"El?" I want to tell her I need help but the words won't form in my mouth. "I just wanted to say . . . hi. See how you're doing."

"I'm fine," she says. "So are Jim and the kids."

My sister and I are, as she says, leaves off a different tree. But I have never disparaged her way of life, except for the sympathy card I sent with the wedding present—a velvet choker—when she married Jim. And she has never said what she sometimes thinks: I am making a mess of my life.

"Well, I'd better go. This is costing you."

"It's only money," she says.

"Do you know how much I love you?"

"I love you too, Jesse."

I hang up the phone, look back at the bartender. "Thanks."

"*De nada.*"

"Can you tell me how far the next town is?"

"*Que?*"

"The next town. How far is it from here?"

"Ten, twenty miles."

I start to explain to him the important difference between ten and twenty miles when you're using your own feet, but instead I go over and sit down at the bar. A hand-lettered sign next to the cash register reads *Tipping is not a city in China.*

"What'll it be?"

"A beer. Anything on draft."

He picks up a glass, pulls down the spigot, slips the lip of the glass just under it, and looks back up at me.

"You in trouble?"

"Trouble? Me? No. Uh-uh."

"Just asking," he says, setting the glass in front of me.

"Thanks."

He smiles, nods his head. Dark curly hair. Nice eyes. Biceps that speak of workouts.

I take the small wad of bills from my back pocket, peel off a twenty.

He holds up his hand. "It's on the house."

The movement of the bus makes the words tremble on the page.

"We'll be stopping in San Francisco in half an hour," the bus driver says. "Those of you who are getting off, please check to make sure you have your personal belongings with you, and thank you for traveling Greyhound. For those continuing on, there'll be a twenty-minute stop. The bus will reboard at exactly twelve o'clock." The microphone clicks off.

"I hope he's there," I hear a woman say, and the man beside me stirs but does not wake. I look at him more closely then—fifty, I'd guess; by the gold ring choking the flesh of his finger, long married; asleep on his own shoulder, at ease in this borrowed space.

I have begun three letters to Lucky on the lined yellow notebook paper I got from the five-and-dime in the last town we stopped at. I was looking for the Arby's but it wasn't where the bus driver said: "Two blocks north, take a right, over the train tracks, a half block left, you can't miss it." People who give you directions always say that. But they're wrong; you can miss it. Everyone on the bus had a fat roast beef sandwich and French fries while there I sat, empty-handed, wondering whether the person who hears a different drummer may not be deaf.

I begin again. *Dear Lucky* . . . What was it I wanted to say? *I'm sorry. I left your car by the side of the road somewhere north of the Blue Light Café.* I wad up the paper, begin again. *Dear Lucky* . . . I try to concentrate but the bathroom door slams against the backseat every three seconds or so. No one shuts it. The lights of an oncoming truck light up the road ahead, then pass. It makes me think of the Mack truck that hit me, and I wonder what became of the driver, or my car, or the notebooks in the trunk. Probably in a junkyard somewhere. Twenty-four years' worth of notebooks, a few paperbacks, some clothes: my life. I wonder if someone, looking for a spare tire, maybe, or a used jack, will find them, and if he does, what he will make of them—some pages written over in different-colored ink, some pages crossed out altogether. At first, I admit, losing those notebooks was a relief—gone, gone, the past in its final place, the way a born-again Baptist must feel, coming up out of the dark water, everything new. But now I think, Twenty-four years gone, what a shame.

This is the only plot. All is lost. Begin again.

I stare at the slightly oily forehead of the man beside me and will him awake.

It begins to rain and the bus driver turns the windshield wipers on. I remember something Lucky said once. "You don't think it's raining unless it hits you."

"That's not true," I whisper to the sleeping man.

I lean my head back against the cushion and stare out the window, but I can see only the reflection of my own face. I put my hand to the place where the handprint was, as if in consolation.

The lights of the Bay Bridge begin as we come into San Francisco.

PART THREE

Black Is Black

In a stall with no door a hefty woman in a paisley print is praying to the toilet. A skinny redhead in stiletto heels, tight Levi's, and a pink bathing suit top comes in, hears the retching, looks down. She says, "I know what you mean." Then she wets a paper towel, folds it in half like a washcloth, and hands it to the woman on her knees. The woman gets up, wipes her lips, walks with unsteady dignity to a sink. We stand there, three strangers in a horizontal mirror. The redhead looks at me. She smiles. Her blue eye shadow crinkles. I begin to cry. No, I howl. She pats my shoulder and says, "It will be all right." Florence Nightingale in the terminal restroom. I smile back, a smile that doesn't make it to my eyes, walk out into the night, unable to see after the harsh lights in the mirror, the retching woman's white face.

I have thirty-four dollars in my three-day dirty pants—what's left from the bus ticket and some miscellaneous expenses: cigarettes, a Snickers, one greasy cheeseburger, coffee. As many dollars as I am old, I think. Pitiful. I figure that will get me two nights in some down and out hotel with enough left over for food if I steal it. Never a great disciple of delayed gratification, I decide to try it. The beach is free.

I walk west on Mission toward the ocean. For a chain-smoker the hills are killers. I walk slowly, repeating her tender words to myself: *It will be all right. It will be all right.* There seemed a certainty in such kindness.

I heard his breathing before I heard his footsteps, heard the two-tone moan of it there in the dark. Then I felt his hand, large and cold, covering my mouth, his thumb pulling down one corner of my eye, the thrill of cold metal against my throat, his breath against my hair, "This will teach you," his arm clenched around me, flattening my breasts, the smell of whiskey and cigarettes, and then that laugh, pure malice, which scared me more than the knife. I tried to scream, choked on it, tried again, his fingers were wet with it, wet with my spit, tightening over me, over my nose, over my mouth. "This will teach you," he whispered again, and then laughed, *"This* will teach you," a tone of triumph now giving style to the malice. I felt myself being dragged backward, cartoon style, straight legged, the heels of my feet skidding along the pavement, socks coming off, a prologue. *No I said no I won't no.* Did I say the words or only think them? Either way he wasn't listening. He was big, six-five, six-six, three hundred fifty pounds at least, a power lifter, overdosed on steroids. I watched him from too close, out of the corner of my eye, as I was being dragged backward; I strained to see him until my eyes teared. He was grunting, grunting hard with the effort, the terrible effort it must have been of wrenching a woman against her will into some dark place, safe from streetlights and sympathy. It was already dark but it got darker still. Black as night in a cellar. I don't know where I was that this should be so, I heard no door opening and closing, no movement from the street to wherever I lay barely breathing. Before this thought was even complete, I felt myself beginning to give up, to desert my body, and I fought against it, bit at his hand covering my mouth, bit my own lips, flapped my arms, which he held pinned to my sides, flapped and flapped like some crippled seal. Then he was hovering above me, a menace of flesh, and I didn't understand the transition, from there to here, how did it go? He forced a knee between my legs, unzipped his pants, then mine, all in one smooth motion, as if he had had lots of practice, as if rape were something he practiced every chance he got. Instead of screaming I laughed. I don't know why, but maybe this: no one should have such an ugly rapist—clumsy, huge, grotesque, a circus animal's face, his breathing even not quite human, catching on something (fear? the smell of death?) before it escaped. I heard myself then, heard myself say, "No, please, no, you don't have to do this, you don't, you're an attractive man, you could have any—" *Slap.* He slapped me, hard. Mean but not gullible, he knew: his face was the assault the world had made on him and it happened every day. He grabbed the front of my clothes then, a wad in one huge hand and ripped, like a magician unveiling his finest trick. Cold, I felt so cold, the cold on my breasts, cold arms, cold at the base of my spine, then his fat crude hands looming, moving erratically, like some deaf-mute giant telling the story of what he would do to me, in sign language. Oh the weight of that man, he nearly flattened the breath out of me. I felt the concrete beneath my back, felt my backbone press into it, each knob of my spine pressed into it so hard that I thought my body would leave a print. And I felt his hand on my hair—smoothing it back—and then, before he touched my skin with his hands, I passed out, abdicated the body, no more myself but an unwilling instrument of pain, simply left, out of cowardice or wisdom, I can't say. So I've had to imagine what he did to me while I was not there, by the evidence he left: a purple moon-shaped slash beneath my left eye (he had on a ring, he must have caught me under the eye with that, but why, when there was no longer any resistance, or maybe it was just that), a bruise beneath my ribs, on the right side (where he lay spent, I suppose, crushing me, trembling perhaps, his sperm oiling my thighs). There were no bruises below the waist. Nothing. Like fucking a dead woman, I thought with satisfaction, that's what it must've been like, and I smiled to myself, glad to have triumphed if only in this, to have deprived him of whatever response he had hoped for—pleading, incomprehension, pain, or all that fear.

"They used to manufacture weapons here," she says, unlocking the door, locking it again behind us, then leading me up the dark stairs. Her name is Louise and she came to get me at the police station, held my hand at the hospital while they examined me again with cold metal instruments, gave me a pill that would kill the rapist's baby before it existed.

We walk into a room furnished with boards and bricks for book-shelves, garish posters on dirty white walls, a floral couch, and two mismatched chairs. A dark-haired woman sits in a cage like the ticket booth at a carnival.

"Jesse, this is Elizabeth."

Elizabeth smiles slightly, then reconsiders, like a pallbearer arranging her face for the trip to the hearse.

On the blackboard behind Elizabeth's head: *Rape is the world's way of telling a woman she can't get away with it.* Someone has crossed out *Rape* and written *Life* above it.

"Jesse will be staying with us for a while," Louise says.

Elizabeth nods vigorously but says nothing, and I wonder what the cage is for—to protect her or us?

"There are some forms to fill out," Louise says, "but that can wait until morning."

She leads me down a dimly lit hall, opens the door to a room with two twin beds, a table with a small round mirror over it, a wooden chair, and an olive green chest of drawers with orange and yellow sunflowers for handles.

"The suite at the Motel 6," Louise says. "The bathroom is through there." She points to a closed door in the corner. "You share it with the woman on the other side."

I look at Louise, my eyes wide. Her too?

She nods, and suddenly I imagine, in small rooms all over this city, all over this country, the world, women in different stages of defeat.

"But not everyone here is a victim of rape. This is also a shelter for battered women and their children."

I nod and smile, as if this were everyday news—how nice.

"There's a nightgown in the top drawer of the dresser and a change of clothes for in the morning. If you want something to read, help yourself to the books in the office. Elizabeth will be there all night. I'm at the end of the hall, in the room on the right, if you want to talk or if you need something to help you sleep." She hugs me quickly and walks out.

I sit on the bed, looking out the window at Ernie's Auto Body Shop, run my hand over the pink chenille bedspread. I unbutton the trench coat the officer loaned me, check the pockets for messages, then hang it up in the closet. Two wire hangers dangle at odd angles from a metal bar, comic, forlorn.

I take off my clothes and try to think what to do with them. There's a metal wastebasket under the table; I stuff them in that, wishing I had a match.

I open the top drawer of the dresser, take out a light blue flannel nightgown. It has long sleeves with lace at the edges of the elastic cuffs, around the neck. Something a child of ten might wear.

I go into the bathroom, turn the water on hot, and wonder about the woman behind the closed door. I let the hot water run in my mouth. I stay in there a long time, until my skin is red, my fingertips withered.

I put the nightgown on, wrap a towel around my wet hair. There's nothing to comb it out with so I leave it tangled. I don't look in the mirror.

I turn off the light in the bedroom and lie down on top of the covers, thinking the pattern of shadows is different in every room. Something you wouldn't know if you'd never left home.

Muffled sounds coming from next door.

"You will have to cry for yourself," Louise said. "You will have to grieve." But I feel strangely peaceful. The world has done its worst. No matter what happens now, I am safe.

In the middle of the night something wakes me. Crying. Not next door, somewhere else. The wail of a child, insistent, heartbroken, as if believing that if she cries loudly enough, someone will come. I hear footsteps down the hall, a door opening and closing. Then silence.

I gave the police a description. "The elephant man," I said. "Look for the elephant man. Only bigger. More grotesque." But the face of the rapist was not in any of the cracked albums of pictures—of drug dealers, murderers, ordinary assaulters with deadly weapons. They asked me again and again what he said, as if they might reconstruct that face from the sound of his voice alone: *This will teach you, this will teach you.* Or maybe they liked the fear in my voice when I said it. Or they might have been thinking of some lesson of their own.

I pull the covers up under my chin, watching the shadow of a moving car traverse the wall, grow steadily larger, then smaller, then disappear. It seems sinister, threatening, but maybe everything after a rape seems threatening.

A rape. Passive. Impersonal. Grammar will not save you.

This will teach you, this will teach you. I say the words over and over, as if by repetition they might yield up their meaning.

I hear the woman next door go into the bathroom, blow her nose. I imagine her looking into the mirror and seeing . . . nothing. She is afraid. Afraid of the dark. And of falling asleep, of what she will dream. But what she is most afraid of is that she will always be afraid. Who is she now that her confidence is shot? What? Not even the illusion of identity is left. The toilet flushes and she returns to her bed but she cannot sleep, I hear her springs creaking, she is turning and turning in her bed.

This will teach you, this will teach you. I put my hands over my ears but the words still come.

I remember something then, a story Lucky told me about his uncle—the one with the dead eyes and pinched lips in Waxahachie, Texas. "My uncle was a religious man," Lucky said, "and when I had done something the Lord didn't love, he would hold my hand over the flame of a candle. To teach me a lesson, is what he said. I never knew what the lesson was, except maybe that human flesh burns."

If I see him again I will tell him: there is a certainty in degradation.

"The policeman asked, Did he hurt you?" She laughs.

"I feel so ashamed." Nodding heads, murmured assent.

"I feel so—I don't know—*lost*. Like somebody died."

I feel like throwing up. The price of admission is being raped, a willingness to confess. Victims Anonymous. I say nothing.

"Did yours have a knife? Did he?" Wild hair, bruised lips. "I want to know. I *must know.*"

Did you fight or lay there quietly, barely breathing, hands like dead things beside you, a shame to your race? We would all like to know.

"It was like I was standing outside my own body, watching. Like watching grown people grow small from the window of the plane. Only I was one of them. I keep thinking . . . If I could get back in. Maybe then . . ."

What? What then?

"Afterwards. After he— He said. He said he was . . . *sorry.*"

A gentleman. And what did you say?

"Even shadows make me afraid now. Nightmares of faceless men. Staying up all night to escape, only to die in dreams in the morning."

"Yes." A trio. Depression in C minor.

"I want to pay the bastard back. To *hurt* him."

Louder this time, a goddamn choir: "*Yessss.*"

"If he didn't have a knife. If only he didn't have a knife. Did yours have a knife?"

"I feel like somebody died. Me."

This is not self-pity. Self-pity presupposes a self.

"So ashamed." Her head jerks, the flinch of some remembered fist.

"He wants to know, did he hurt me?" She laughs, the joke of the year.

"It's been over a month now, but I can still feel his breath on my face."

Whiskey and cigarettes.

"I take a shower three times a day. I scrub myself with Lysol. With *Lysol.* But no matter how hard I scrub, he's still there. *On* me." She shudders, hugs her arms to her breasts, what is left of her.

"Jesse?" It's Louise.

"I don't like public confessionals."

Did yours have a knife? turns on me. "Why, lady? Why'd you come then?"

Silent, stoical, superior. The feeling comes and goes: an impostor in my own clothes.

She snorts at me, leaves me looking at the back of her head, shades of reddish orange and bleached blond going to black at the crown.

"The policeman said, Did he hurt you?" She holds her clenched fists between her knees, elbows straight, wrists together—as if we were supposed to guess which hand had the answer.

"You will have to cry for yourself," Louise says. "You will have to grieve."

Tonight is our first lesson. There are seven of us here, eight counting Louise, who runs the shelter. We are to gather together once a week, a kind of memorial, I guess, for those whose funerals have preceded their demise, whose lives came undone in the unsuspecting streets, the floor of a friend of a friend's apartment with a view of South Bay, an elevator stalled on its way to the top—Who could have predicted it?—in the alley behind the Ritz Café after a meal of blackened redfish and new potatoes, in a parking lot in North Beach, in broad daylight, on the front seat of an unlocked car, the lasting impression of a gearshift, between the stacks on the sixth floor of the library at San Francisco State, a late reader, here at home, on white sheets. The story is different but the ending is always the same: none will escape. No matter how many times the story is told, which one the teller, she, I, you, we will not find the simple extraordinary fact—a course in karate, a buttoned blouse, the bandanna tighter against the head, the purposeful stride—that will make the impossible possible, that will give us back ourselves.

"I . . ." It is me, surprised into speech.

No one speaks. They are wary, waiting. And they're right to be wary. I don't trust them. I don't intend to tell them anything.

"Jesse?" It's Louise.

I look down at my hands, as if there were crib notes for living. I choke on my own spit, try to begin.

"Maybe next time," Louise says.

I get halfway up out of my chair, look for the door. I don't belong here. I don't have anything in common with these women.

Did yours have a knife? looks at me and nods her head. "Maybe next time," she says and smiles carefully, ready to take it back if she's rejected, but she keeps looking at me steadily until I sit down.

"Tonight we are going to discuss the topic of guilt," Louise says.

I decide to stay, listen. It can't hurt to listen.

"When it happened to me, I thought it was my fault," Louise says, raising her arms as if against some oppression of the air. "It was not."

Everyone nods, tentatively, looking around. We would all like to believe her, ourselves.

"Repeat after me. *It was not my fault.*"

We do as she says. Maybe it won't help but what is the alternative? Remembering? Rehearsing it? Here is where you made your fatal mistake, here is where you should have struggled, screamed, fallen silent, begged, kissed your rapist as requested.

Their voices wash over me, indistinct, but just being like this, in the presence of women, is . . . comforting. I don't have to look behind me. This is what I think, and the thought startles me—that I have always been looking behind me—something I wouldn't have known except by its contrast.

I blink, trying to see the face of the speaker more clearly. I haven't been out of this dimly lit building since I was led into it more than a week ago. I think of the blind singer at the Stoneleigh P being led onto the stage, and I wonder again what became of her. Can a person die of blindness? Or maybe she got tired of the dark.

"Next time we'll talk about grief," Louise says, and the meeting is over, the women get up out of their chairs, stand around looking at one another, awkward, confused, not knowing where or what. Then Louise begins to herd us, a hand on the back, an open door. We shuffle down the hall to our rooms, already old.

I close the door behind me, lie down on top of the pink chenille bedspread. What was it she said? Did yours have a knife?

To me these women have no names. *Did yours have a knife? Did he hurt me? Somebody died. With Lysol. So ashamed. If I could get back in* . . . That's what I think of as their names. Just the lines they repeat, over and over. Except for Louise. She is real to me. Why? Maybe because she reminds me of my mother, the same green eyes, damaged and kind. Her father was a bruiser.

I put on the light blue nightgown and see an image of my own father standing beside my bed, whispering, "The End." I start to cry then, feel newly abandoned. When something very bad happens to you, every bad thing that has ever happened to you happens again. At eighty, think of it. If we didn't die of old age we would die of grief.

The One True Story of the World.

I start to laugh, a violent sound like clothes ripping. I laugh so loudly that several people come running. I fall on my knees laughing.

"It's okay," Louise says, "it's okay," stroking my hair, rocking me, a full-grown child in a stranger's nightgown.

"He smoothed my hair," I say, puzzled, as if this were the clue that would solve the crime. But she doesn't say anything, even when

I repeat it. "He smoothed my hair." As if she had not heard me or as if I had not spoken.

Somewhere, in one of the rooms, Carole King is singing, and I wonder what year it is, what city I am in, what crime I have committed. Where is my mother?

I have been wounded in an accident and there is no way I can undo it. These are the words I repeat to myself, over and over, as if truth were an antidote to suffering.

On the fifteenth day I get up out of bed and make myself a promise. Today I will go out into the world. Alone. Fearless. My old self.

I put on a shirt for a robe and, without combing my hair, go to the kitchen, eat breakfast alone. It is almost noon. Everyone else has been up for hours. After breakfast, where do they go? I have black coffee and toast, dry toast. Anything else makes my stomach queasy, as if I were pregnant.

I laugh out loud, scattering toast crumbs into the air. Wouldn't that be wonderful? Some little bastard to look at every day for the rest of your life who is a miniature version of the man who made you forever afraid. Or maybe some touching combination of the two: his gruesome face, your cowering eyes.

Then the thought comes: it might be Lucky's. I might be pregnant with Lucky's child. Would I keep it then? If it were his?

After breakfast I take two sleeping pills and go back to bed.

When I wake up the next afternoon the world is still there. I sit on the edge of the bed, dangle my bare feet, feel lighter than normal, as if during the night I had lost substance. I get a glimpse of my face in the mirror over the chest of drawers: wild eyes, wilder hair. I look in all the drawers for a comb or a brush, then in the bathroom. Nothing.

I knock gently on the door to the adjoining room. I hear footsteps, feel sudden fear. *Be calm. There is nothing to be afraid of. Someone is coming because you knocked.* I speak to myself as to a disturbed and fragile child.

Did yours have a knife? opens the door.

I gesture to my hair. "Do you have a comb or a brush?" Looking at her bleached blond hair sticking out every which way, it seems a silly question to ask, but she nods, opens the door wide. When I don't move forward she takes my hand, leads me into the room, sits me down on the straight-backed chair in front of her mirror. She takes a brush from the top drawer, begins to brush my hair, being careful to untangle it gently, careful not to hurt me.

I start to cry. "When you're like this," I explain to the woman in the mirror, "the smallest kindness can undo you."

She nods but doesn't comment; she just keeps brushing, humming a little under her breath, like my mother used to do while she French-braided my hair, so tightly it made my eyes slant. After most of the tangles are out and my hair is still flyaway, bent, going in every direction, she gets a spray bottle from the bathroom, sprays my hair with a fine mist, and then brushes it dry. When she's through I look almost human, though not like anyone I recognize.

"My name is Sheila," she says, setting the brush down and putting out her hand.

"Jesse," I say, taking her hand. Then, touching my hair, "Thank you."

She looks at me for a moment, as if weighing the sincerity of this remark, and finally nods.

"I haven't been out of this building since I came into it over two weeks ago," I say. "Will you go for a walk with me to the beach?" We're on Nineteenth and something, only blocks from the ocean.

"Okay," she says doubtfully, twisting a lock of bleached blond hair.

"Are you afraid?"

"I'm afraid," she says. Then she arches her eyebrows and moves her eyes back and forth, cartoon scared.

We look at each other and laugh.

"Come on," I say, and she hooks her arm inside my arm. We're like two drunks, neither of which can stand alone but who, holding each other up, somehow manage to make it home.

"We're going for a walk," I tell Elizabeth at the front desk. She purses her lips, half nods, as if she could not pronounce on the wisdom of this.

We walk down the stairs. The door slams behind us and we both jump, then laugh at ourselves. "What a couple of fraidy-cats," Sheila says.

The light is so bright on the concrete pavement that I squint my eyes. We walk along without talking, unsure of each other, unsure of the day. Each breath I take is conscious, measured, shallow, my body no longer my own but an object in the world. There is something shameful in being so vulnerable.

When we're seven or eight blocks from the ocean, I can see where the darker blue of the water meets the blue of the sky. "This is where I was headed when . . . it happened. I guess I finally made it," I say and laugh. "The hard way."

"I'm not interested in anybody who's had an easy life," Sheila says, opening one hand matter-of-factly. "They're white bread. The first thing I want to know about you is what you've suffered and what you know because of it. If nobody ever hit you in the mouth, for instance, you might by accident say something true but you wouldn't *know* it."

I take this speech as an odd attempt at consolation.

"It isn't enough, of course. You might have gotten all the sense knocked out of you."

I laugh.

"Take Jack, my first husband. He tried to. Knock the sense out of me, I mean. Said I deserved it because of my mouth. Said my mouth would get me killed one of these days. What do you think?"

I think she means to suggest that we are both members of some club. "I hope he's wrong."

"I'm still kicking," she says and flips a bird to the imagined Jack.

"Look at that," I say. A dark-haired man is hitting a woman—she has long blond hair—in the back of the head on the front lawn of a pink stucco house. I look at Sheila and there is fear in her eyes.

"What should we do?" she asks.

I start to walk in their direction, but I hesitate. She touches my arm.

Then the blond woman turns around and it's a man. I feel sick, as if someone had duped me, made me think it was a woman being beaten up when all along it was somebody who could take care of himself. But maybe he couldn't. Maybe that was the lesson in the assault. The blond starts to run down the sidewalk toward the ocean; he is barefoot. Soon his body is lost in the sun. The dark-haired man curses and goes back inside, slams the door.

"This rapist," Sheila says, walking again. "He didn't know it but next to my husband he was strictly small time. As far as pain goes." She dances back and forth, shadowboxing the air.

"Sure," I say, but I don't believe the bravado. I am filled with regret that I didn't try to help the woman, or the man I thought was a woman, or even the man.

"What about you?" she says.

"What about me what?"

"Were you ever married?"

"Once," I say.

"What happened?"

I look up and there is another man coming toward us. He's about six feet tall, two hundred pounds, big enough to do us damage. I see Sheila flinch, and my heart begins to pound wildly. I put my arm around her shoulder. "It will be all right," I say, but I don't believe this either. When he gets within strangling distance I close my eyes.

"What a nervous Nellie," she says when the man has passed. "Whew!" She wipes imaginary sweat from her forehead and flings it down.

I laugh. "If we weren't so pathetic we would be comic."

"A couple of real sissies," she says.

I think of my father. *Make a fist. Like this. Now make your will just like that fist. When you've got it right, you won't cry.*

"Maybe we should set ourselves some easy tests," I say. "Work up to these things slowly."

"Good idea," she says. Then she is lost in thought for several blocks, and I notice how these pink and blue and green houses are jammed together, not even an inch between them. I wonder whether when someone is beaten up in one house you can hear it in the next and the next, growing fainter.

"Okay," Sheila says. "First test. Go out alone in broad daylight. That's something I think I can handle."

I nod in agreement. "Second test," I say, after another block. "Talk to a man in an ordinary tone of voice. Without your hands shaking."

"Yeah," she says. "I could use some instruction in that. I lost my job last Tuesday, the first day back. A man came in and asked for a maple bar. When I went to hand it to him, my hand shook so bad I dropped it on the floor, frosting side down, and started to bawl."

"Were you a waitress?"

"Donut hostess," she says, rolling her eyes.

I laugh and shake my head. Then, so as not to have appeared disrespectful, I ask, "Do you miss it?"

"The job? Getting up at four-thirty in the morning? Thirty-seven sickening kinds of donuts? 'Would you like anything from our Dobey's Donut Topping Bar, sir or madam?' Nope. There's no future in donuts."

I don't know her well enough yet to know that this is low-class irony. "Back to the tests," I say. "The third thing." I clear my throat. "The third thing we have to do is apply for a job. Where there are men. Because there are men everywhere."

"We could join a convent," she says, a question in her voice. She studies me a moment, as if imagining me in a black habit, a prayer book in my hands, and then shakes her head. "Nah. I guess we're not convent material," she says.

I smile, thinking how much I like her.

"And for the last test . . ." She puts a finger to her purpled lips, considering. "I've got it. Go out walking after midnight." She looks at me for confirmation.

I nod. That's the real test—where the dark holds everything you can imagine.

"We can do it together, right? Or would that be cheating?" She twirls a finger around and around a lock of blond hair, twists her mouth to the left side of her face.

"There's a difference between courage and stupidity."

"Yes," Sheila says. "If only we knew what it is." And we walk down the stone steps to the sea.

To our right is the Cliff House, and beneath the Cliff House, on a lower level, there's a small white building with a sign over the door. WELCOME TO THE CAMERA OBSCURA. An old man is standing at the door, wearing an apron, a money changer strapped to his belt. His face looks like somebody stood on it all night wearing waffle-soled shoes.

"It's late," he says, "the sun's going down, but I think you can still get the effect. I'll let you ladies go in for a buck each." He jerks a thumb over his shoulder.

Neither of us asks what the effect is or where we are going. We're both thinking the same thing: this is our man. All we have to do is say something without trembling.

I take my money out of my pocket and peel off two one-dollar bills, give them to the man, hands shaking like a drunk going cold turkey.

"You won't regret it," he says.

I look him straight in the eyes, clasping my hands together, holding them tightly against my ribs. "Thank you," I say, as proud as an autistic child of her first sentence.

"My pleasure," he says, and all the wrinkles in his face rise in a smile.

"Thank you," Sheila says.

"My pleasure," he says again and stands back, gestures us inside.

We look through the door, wary, two timid sisters at Halloween. The walls are covered with holographs—a sailboat, a skull—suspended in green eerie light.

We step farther into the room, pitch-dark except for the small circle of light coming in from above. I move to the center of the room and peer into what looks like a huge wok, painted white, about waist level, with a periscope attached that goes up through the roof into the sky. The periscope reflects the real world onto the white surface, but at a fraction of the size; the moving world, not a static image. Amazed, I watch the infinitesimal sea gulls fly. I reach out my huge hand and touch them.

"Look at that," Sheila says, then covers up the sun, pointing. She is standing on the other side, across from me, her face lit by the whiteness, her eyes deep in shadow.

I look at where she's pointing. What I see are two people on top of Seal Rock. They are kissing. They look like tiny human dolls. About an inch high. We both laugh. It is touching, ridiculous.

I can see the world in that convex lens, the tiniest waves coming in, the miniature sun going down. "Now I know what it feels like to be God," I say and think of the woman in the shelter who is standing outside her own body, watching.

"Those two lovers," Sheila says, "you could take your thumb and middle finger and just flick them off of that rock." She demonstrates.

How fragile we are, I think. How stupid and small. I look up at Sheila, but I still can't see her eyes. She points again. Her hand is moon-white on the darkening water.

"What?" I don't know what she's pointing at.

"Right there."

I look down at my own hands, the heel of each palm on the beach, the fingers traversing the ocean. She puts her hands on top of mine. No, she seems to say. This is our true size. I feel my heart beating in my neck. I stare at our hands for a long time, transposed on that horizon, the diminished waves moving under our fingers, as if to soothe them.

"If I'd kicked him hard where he lives or cried out or even begged, *No please no, I am a person, like you, afraid,* or if the moon had been brighter on the concrete pavement, closer than it was to where I lay, or if the streetlight had come before the corner, or if the people passing by had not already seen this movie too many times, the reluctant lover, the part where Kim Basinger is gagged and stripped, the camera pans, catches the secret smile, it's all in the eyes—*Does this excite you? Yes*—or simply as an element of surprise the woman is knifed in the shower and will never come clean, a classic, or this, listen to this, this really happened. Remember Kitty Genovese, the scene where she crawls away from the maniac for the second time, morally wounded but not yet without a will, toward the back door of the apartment building where she might still live—New York it was, in Queens, I think—where the doorman waits for his shift to end and thirty-eight stand watching, waiting, too, for the swell of music that signals the climax, the hero's imminent entrance, the flashy rescue, revenge at the very least? Well, it wasn't a movie and the only one who came back for her was the guy with the knife."

"And how was it for you, when you were raped?" Louise asks, the harsh word put gently, nodding her head in encouragement.

I recount the details slowly—the details of violence are easiest to recall—the hands from behind, the cold metal against my throat, the smell of whiskey and cigarettes, and the laugh, I will never forget that laugh, or the words he repeated again and again—*This will teach you, this will teach you*—or the terrible weight of that man, the concrete beneath my bare back, him smoothing my hair, strange gentleness, and then the blacking out. "I always thought I'd die first, before I'd . . . I didn't."

Sheila puts her hand on my shoulder. The others come, one by one.

"What happens happens," Louise says, and her voice has that sudden vibrato I have come to recognize in my own.

A sound rises in the room; it rises higher, changes key, like a choir in the back ward of the asylum, or the sound coyotes make when the moon is right, first one, then another of us, and another, until every woman in the room is crying, for herself and for the others, and will not be comforted.

"Did he *hurt* me?" Dianne asks.

I say, "Yes. He hurt you." There is nothing she did not suffer, no; nor we. I take her in my arms and rock her. I say it, over and over. "Yes, he hurt you, yes." I know, more than most, the temptations of self-pity. This is not self-pity. Everything is what it is and not another thing.

The Animal Shelter is a bar on the coast, about fifteen minutes south of San Francisco, run by a former veterinarian named Monte, who is taller than most men, a master at liars' dice, drinks Cajun martinis, and who did not ask for a résumé of my triumphs and defeats when I applied for the job of bartender he had advertised in the *Guardian*.

When I walked into the bar that first afternoon, Patsy Cline was singing "I Fall to Pieces" and I felt right at home. I told him what I wanted, and he asked his one and only question: "Are you good with your hands?"

I said I was and he asked me to make him a drink, which I did, hands trembling only slightly as I shoveled the ice into the metal shaker, poured the Tanqueray over it, moved the shaker slowly around in the air, then strained the gin into a long-stemmed glass. I saw him smile when the last drop of gin was the last drop the glass would hold, then I speared a hot pepper with a toothpick and wondered whether I'd lose the job when the pepper sank and the gin overflowed.

"I like mine straight, honey," he said, pulling the pepper off the toothpick just before it touched the rim. He ate it in one bite, threw the stem on the bar, then drank the gin in three equal gulps. Fire and ice.

"You're the only one so far who knows the meaning of a Cajun martini," he said. "If you can learn not to flinch when a customer calls you honey, the job's yours. It pays five an hour plus tips, no drinking behind the bar. Be back at six o'clock."

I said if I could do that I would, thanked him, and walked out, down along Esplanade, south toward the pier, thinking how a single gesture or a phrase can bring back the past so nearly whole, so nearly complete in its details of image and voice and touch that the body reacts as if in the presence of the real thing—the heart pounds, the hands ache, and the rush of blood through the veins is indistinguishable from desire.

Today is only the second time since I moved into the women's shelter that I've been out during the day, and the sun is so bright on the water, I have grown so accustomed to the dim light of the rooms, that I have to close my eyes and open them again slowly.

The shore is lined with fishermen, ten or twelve—rubber boots to their knees, casting lines into the moving water, the waves causing them to sway slightly on their feet. I stand and watch for a while, the sun feeling good on my pale skin, the way a convalescent must feel, coming out into the bright day after bedridden months of tea and toast, ratty hair, rumpled sheets. I wonder where Lucky is, if he thinks of me, and if he does, whether his thoughts are of longing or relief. I hope that he is unhappy, that he feels the lack of me as great, inconsolable, and can no longer imagine a world in which I do not figure.

Some people are doomed to be always leaving a place, as if they existed only in the moment of change, as if nothing were abiding but always passing away: this thought, a dream lost on waking, a framed photograph cracked under the heel of their going. I was one, one of those homeless people—not in the ordinary sense of having no place to hang a favorite robe or sit down to supper, but as a restlessness deeper than anyone knows; one of those people whose homelessness is innate, as if they were born not knowing where or what, cursed with a nostalgia for a place they'd never been, for someone else's past, you could say, though the words are inexact. And so I am surprised—no, amazed—at the desire rising inside me, a desire as of hunger or of thirst, so immediate and physical in its hold that it seems not a desire I have but that it has me: to go home, wherever that might be, to find all those loved and lost waiting, saying, You have come so far, now it is over.

I stand a while longer looking out at the water, blue then darker blue going to gray, watching the waves in their continual falling, the fishermen swaying, keeping their difficult balance.

Wherever You Go, There You Are

My mother sits sewing at the kitchen table. She presses her foot down hard on the pedal, pushing the material under the needle so fast that it jams. "Shit!" she says, slapping the top of the wheel several times to turn it back, gouging out the stitches with a small forklike object. She smooths the blue material with her hands, repositions it under the needle, begins again.

The machine makes a noise for which I am grateful. She doesn't expect me to talk. The topic we are not discussing is why I have come.

I study the fragile line of her bent neck, the long gray hair pulled all to one shoulder, and think how age makes even a strong person seem vulnerable.

"Shit!" she says again, destroying the illusion. Then, trying for a casual tone, "So what have you been doing out there in that barn?"

I wasn't *in* the barn. I only made it to the double doors. "Just looking."

"Looking for what? There's nothing to look at out there but ghosts. Why go dragging up the past, making new wounds out of old?"

"I was wondering about the boat."

"Wondering what? If it'll float? Well, I can save you the trouble. It won't," she says, turning the wheel back, yanking the blue material out, jabbing at it with the ripper.

"If it might be restored."

"The hull is rotted clear through," she says. "*Restored* sounds like the wrong word, if you ask me."

"Okay. Rebuilt."

"What for? The last I heard you were scared to go near the water. Remember that time at Pine Crest?" She laughs. "I thought your little knees were going to beat each other to death."

She is right. I am afraid of large bodies of water in general, drowning in particular. "A person can change," I say in my defense.

She looks at me sceptically but goes on with her sewing.

"What are you making?" I ask, to change the subject.

"A mess," she says and laughs. "Actually it's a winter coat."

A winter coat she will find, half-finished, in some forgotten drawer come spring.

She looks at me like she knows what I'm thinking. "That's enough ripping out for today," she says, doing a backstitch, flipping the needle lever up; she takes the material out, bites off the loose thread, folds it.

"Tonight's my bingo. Can you fix yourself some dinner? There's leftover stew in the refrigerator and some homemade beer bread wrapped in foil in the cupboard over the stove."

"I'll be fine, Mama. I've been fixing my own dinner for several years."

"Yes. I keep forgetting. You're all grown-up now with mistakes of your own."

I let this pass, more from weariness than tact.

She starts to leave the room but then turns back. "Will you be here when I get home?"

"Yes."

"How long will you be staying for this time? If you don't mind my asking."

"Just until Sunday night. I've got a new job. I told you."

"Oh, yes. A veterinarian's assistant, was it?"

"Something like that."

"Well, I hope it lasts longer than the last one," she says, walking out of the room before I can answer.

I get a beer from the refrigerator and take it into the living room, sit down at the old upright. Above me, in a gold leaf frame, my sister plays some song I can't remember in a white silk dress, her long slender fingers poised above the keys, looking out at the same scene I see from where I sit: the circular driveway, the creek that dissects the far field where the oak tree stands with its two long low-lying branches, one on each side, like human arms, that we used to ride on as children.

I play the first few bars of "Mad about Him Sad about Him How Can I Be Glad without Him Blues," a song my father used to like, boogie-woogie. The piano is seriously out of tune.

My mother comes out of the bedroom transformed—bright lipstick, her long hair up, smelling of lilac.

"You sure you're just going to play bingo?"

She laughs self-consciously and looks twenty years younger. "Now don't go getting any ideas," she says. "I'm an old woman." But she laughs again and I know she is trying to convince herself. "You can come if you want to. There's a $2,500 jackpot. You might get lucky."

I flinch at the name as if struck.

"Did I say something? I'm sorry. I thought you might want . . ."

"It's all right, Mama. I'm just touchy lately." For the last thirty-four years.

"Well, if you're sure you won't come . . ."

"I think I'll just stay here and drink," I say, raising my beer bottle.

"Suit yourself," she says, making her eyes small, her lips thin.

"You look pretty," I say, and her face changes. "Have a good time."

"I will," she says, pulling the belt of her short gray coat tight around her waist. "I just wish I didn't have to wear this old thing." She shrugs, rattles her car keys in farewell, walks toward the door, opens it, then looks back. She wants to tell me something but she does not.

"Have a good time," I repeat.

She nods and pulls the door closed behind her.

I open the piano bench to see if there's any sheet music inside. Bach's *Two- and Three-Part Inventions.* I take the book out, turn to the first page, study the gold star at the top, the hand-drawn scroll with the date of Ellen's lesson written inside it: June 19, 1962, exactly twenty-five years ago.

My fingers fumble for the right notes and the melody, played at half speed, sounds more melancholy than it should. Ellen was the real musician in the family; I was only a mediocre student. But my mother tried hard to teach me, before I could read—putting strips of adhesive tape on the keys, with numbers printed on them, the same numbers written in again over the notes in the music. "Für Elise" was the first piece she tried to teach me—much too difficult for a beginner—and I would bang my forearms down on the keys and cry because I couldn't make it sound like Ellen could. "Is that any way to treat Furry Lisa?" my mother would ask. "Play it for me," I begged. Shaming me with her eyes, her mouth an unforgiving line, she would say, "No. You must learn to do it yourself"—placing my finger on the first note of the piece—"You will have to go slowly"—tapping the time with her right foot and her forefinger—"Now begin again"—nodding her head.

The cedar chest is still at the foot of their bed, its dark red wood rubbed smooth. I open the lid carefully, its creak a warning: at any moment she will come home to find a shivering child in her room without permission.

I take it out, its dark green cover split, dull with dust, the words *Our Family* in gold and missing gold, the cursive script they teach you in second grade. The pictures are stuck together, and I pry them apart with my fingers, turn the black pages slowly, until I come to the one I want.

Four of the pictures on the page are black, all taken by me. Two are good snapshots of my father but his face has been burned out of them—by my mother, I think, though I have never asked.

My father gave me a camera, a Brownie Instamatic, for my tenth birthday, with the provision that I not take his picture. He said the Kwakiutl Indians believed that to take a person's picture was to steal his soul, and that he was a Kwakiutl by belief if not by birth.

So I learned to be sly.

The first shot was of him sleeping. I set the alarm for three A.M., sure that though he often sat up late, guarding the dark, he would be asleep by then. I took my camera from under the covers, checked to make sure that the small red square in front showed a *1,* then walked without making a sound down the dark hall, my finger on the trigger. I turned the doorknob slowly, like someone opening a safe, then stood in the light of the cheap quartz clock beside their bed. I could see my father through the eye of the camera, but my mother's face was outlined above his nose, so I moved to the foot of the bed to get a better angle. As I heard the two-tone click in the darkness, he shuddered in his sleep, and I imagined the soul's escape from the body, what his eyes would look like in the morning.

At breakfast I was relieved to see him smile at me as always, touch my hair, and whisper, "Jesse, today we will finish the boat that will take us from the pond in the woods to the sea." At ten I knew such promises would not be kept, but the words were more ritual than literal truth, and it gave me a chance to study his eyes above the silver dollar pancakes my mother made on Saturday mornings. When I found no perceptible difference in them, I promised someone somewhere that I would take no more pictures of my father.

The second picture showed an increase of courage or deviousness. It was taken the next evening at dusk when he was working on the wind machine he was building out back, at the northeast corner of the house, near the grape arbor. I took the picture from inside the garage, wiping the dirty four-paned window with the oil-can rag before I clicked the shutter.

I can see the wind machine, almost in shadow, turning slightly in the breeze, my father's head outlined against the blades, a metal headdress, the four panes of the garage window making his face look like part of a puzzle.

After taking the picture I put the camera in my bedroom, beneath the underwear in the top dresser drawer, then went out to see the damage that was done.

"How's it going?" I asked.

"This," he explained, pointing to a rusted bolt attached to a crude circle of plywood, "is for stability." He spun the contraption to give me the idea. There was the scrape of metal on metal, a groaning sound. "A few more refinements," he said and smiled. When he began to talk about wind speed and kilowatts per hour I was satisfied: except for the darkening circles beneath his eyes, he was my father, unchanged.

The one of him standing on the deck of the boat in the barn is one of my favorites. It is shaped like a porthole, and his face, if I remember it right, has the look of a man who has settled something with himself.

After taking the picture through the bubble window on the deck, I hid inside the boat for hours, or that's what it seemed, until he finished sanding the deck, and I heard him jump down to the ground, walk back toward the house. That night, at dinner, I noticed that his left eye had begun to twitch.

I swore I would stop but I couldn't. The fourth picture I got by following him at a distance of thirty yards when he went for a walk in the woods, as he often did on Sunday mornings while my mother was in church. In the middle of the woods is a clearing, and in the middle of the clearing is a pond, shaped like a keyhole, with a large circle of water at the top and a narrow inlet at the bottom, with a small pier—maybe ten feet long—jutting out into the water at the east side of its largest part. He is standing at the end of the pier, looking down. I can still hear the hiss of his cigarette dropped into the pond, the way air sounds escaping an inner tube. I want to call out to him but I do not.

In the fifth picture he is standing by the Packard, one foot on the running board, his right arm raised like a weightlifter or a conqueror. It looks like a picture to which he must have consented, unless my mother got the shot while he was showing off for us kids. I don't remember taking it. There is still a trace of dark hair around the edges of the burned hole. The black from the next page shows through, and the effect is disconcerting, as if someone had stolen his face.

He told us that the old black Packard could fly over railroad tracks. If he pressed a certain button, marked *F,* and if we shut our eyes tight, put our hands over our hearts, believed, it would fly. That's what he said. But when we opened our eyes, there we were on the same side of the tracks, waiting like everyone else for the train to pass. I blamed Ellen and David but never myself.

The sixth picture, taken from a distance, is definitely my mother's fault; it's one taken earlier in the year—of him on the harvester in the field of alfalfa, me beside him. I remember the smell of cut hay, his dark brown arms, the dust streaking his face, but mostly I think of the roar of the machine that drowned out our voices. If I wanted to tell him something, I would put my hands over my ears, as if this would help, put my face an inch from his face, and scream whatever couldn't wait for lunch or sundown. "What Jesse? I can't hear you!" he'd yell. I would only mouth the words then, my lips a dumb show, so he would do what I wanted: turn off the key. When the coughing of the engine had stopped, he would look at me with fond disgust and say, "What? What did you say, Jesse? This better be good."

I put the picture album back in the cedar chest, close the top, reposition the white lace cloth. I stand up, try to approximate the bearing of someone with courage, but I get a glimpse of my face in the dresser mirror: dark shadows under the eyes, a study in guilt or fear.

I heat up some stew in the microwave, butter a piece of home-made bread, open another beer. The air around my head feels heavy, as in waking after a dream. When I'm finished eating, I look at the clock over the sink, its ticking louder than normal. Only ten to seven. Early. Not yet dark.

I look out the back picture window over the dining room table, look toward the barn, see the sun setting behind it, the trapdoor open, the mast of the boat rising up through it. I drop the beer bottle on the table, catch it before it spills, set it upright. I carry my dish to the sink and wash it, dry it, put it away.

The dark is settling over the house, and the furniture in the living room is cast in shadow. It's twilight, the time of day when uncertainty claims everything; even the edges of ordinary objects are unclear. I sit in the corner of the couch, my feet tucked up under me, and try to imagine that Christmas day, the child I was.

Almost twenty-five years later I still walk toward it, the terror rising like vomit, across the salt-grass hills, along the creek, toward the barn, to the place where the unfinished boat still stands, its wooden hull rotted, its keel sunk in mud, the mast rising high above the loft through the barn's trapdoor, where a shaft of moonlight enters . . .

I begin again—walking more quickly this time, with more resolution. I open the double doors wide, see the boat, the mast rising up through the barn's trapdoor; I climb the rope ladder up the side of the boat to the deck, open the hatch.

Again and again I approach and retreat. But that's as far as I get, even in my imagination.

When my mother comes home, I'm still sitting in the living room in the corner of the couch.

She comes in, flips on the light. "Jesus Christ!" she says. "You nearly scared me to death."

"Sorry. How was bingo? Did you win anything?"

"Only a few pull-tabs," she says. "Fifty dollars. No big deal." She hangs up her coat in the closet just inside the front door, shuts it, turns around. "So. What have you been doing besides brooding over things that can't be changed?"

I get up and walk across the room, stand by the piano, as if I would sing.

"I brought us some Baskin-Robbins," she says, closing the door to the coat closet, holding up the white bag. "Your favorite. Pralines 'n' cream."

"That was nice of you."

She takes the bag into the kitchen, and I can hear her scooping the ice cream into two dishes. She carries them out, hands one to me.

"Thanks," I say, still standing.

"So," she says again. But we eat the ice cream in silence, no sound except for the scrape of metal against glass.

"It's good," I say when I'm finished. "Thanks."

"I didn't make it," she says, as if defending herself against some unfair charge.

"No."

She clicks on the TV with her remote control. "Let's see what there is to watch," she says. " 'Lifestyles of the Rich and Famous.' How about that? Maybe they'd like to come and photograph this showplace. Maybe they'd like a shot of my wooden ducks." She laughs, clicks to another channel. " 'Spenser: For Hire.' He's gotten fat." *Click.* She talks herself out of several other possibilities and then settles on a rerun of "Columbo."

I sit down beside her, try to keep my attention on the murder, the details that will be important later. But none of it makes any sense—something about a magician's trick with a guillotine that ends in a man's death.

"I'm going to bed," I say, though the body is still warm.

"Suit yourself," she says, not looking up from the TV. "You always do."

"Good night, Mama," I say from the edge of the room.

She looks up. "Good night. Sleep tight. Don't let the bedbugs bite. If they do, take a shoe, and knock them cuckoo." She laughs. "You used to love that."

"Still do." I walk over and give her a kiss on the cheek. "See you in the morning."

When I get in bed I can't sleep. The room is cool and the stained glass lamp above the bed hovers, makes me wonder if I will, like the magician, be decapitated before morning. I turn in the bed, restless, yank the covers up to my neck, shiver. I close my eyes tight, try to imagine the waves breaking at Pedro Point, relax one muscle at a time, all the tricks I know for the seduction of sleep. I get up and choose a book from the shelf beside the bed. But I can't concentrate and I set it on the nightstand. I hear a coyote somewhere far off and think of the skulls my brother and I sometimes found out in the field, bleached skeletons of small animals, thinking them skulls of Indians, early settlers, skeletons of children like ourselves.

I hear water running in the bathroom, then my mother's footsteps into her room. It is 11:05. I watch the green luminous numbers of the clock move toward 12:00. I try until midnight and then get up, pull on my jeans there on the floor beside the bed, a shirt, some tennis shoes of my mother's, and go to the coat closet. The door is stuck and I am afraid to make too much noise trying to open it, so I settle for my mother's heavy sweater from the back of her sewing-machine chair.

I walk out the back door, careful not to let the screen door slam, move carefully through the dark toward the barn, feeling the foxtails gather in my socks. Moonlight falls on the bridge across the creek, and from there on I know the way by heart.

I open the doors with both hands, open them out, step inside. There is an impression of dampness, cold, something rotten. I climb up the rope ladder on the side of the boat. A shaft of moonlight enters through the open trapdoor, a square of light like a snapshot of the teak deck that creaks with my weight. I open the hatch, go down the ladder slowly, backward, down, into the shallow cabin too shallow now to stand up in. Cobwebs of angel hair cover my eyes. I find my way with my hands, strike a wet match to a rusted lantern that casts an arc of light on the berth like a womb at the fore of the boat then goes out.

Dark, it is dark down here, but I know what I came for: a note with my name on it, a message in the empty bottle of Scotch, a late entry in the logbook, something—to tell me how the story ends.

That Christmas morning there was a present on the nightstand beside my bed, wrapped in silver paper, probably tinfoil from the drawer beside the refrigerator, something my father had rigged up in the middle of the night, having forgotten to buy wrapping paper. I ripped it open. It was a plain gray notebook, about seven inches by nine, with a thick cardboard cover, wide-lined pages sewn in. At the top of the first page, written in black ink, in my father's hand: THE ONE TRUE STORY OF THE WORLD. I looked at the next page, thinking he had written the story down. Nothing. I looked at the back of the book. Then I took the notebook and held it up by one corner of the cover and shook it, hoping something would fall out. Nothing. I looked under the bed, thinking maybe there was a card that had fallen in the dark; I yanked my nightgown up over my knees so I could bend down more easily, tearing it. Nothing. I looked behind the night-stand, the wooden floor cold, feeling the hairs on my bare legs rising. Then I knew, with a certainty no evidence could touch, that some-thing had happened to my father, that he wouldn't have given me that notebook if he was going to be around to keep telling the story.

I pulled on my jeans, stuffed my nightgown inside them, yanked on my tennis shoes without bothering to tie them, and ran out of the house, carrying the notebook, ran across the bridge, toward the barn, opened the double doors. The sailboat was still there. He wouldn't have gone without that. That's the way he always said he would go. I climbed down into the boat to make sure he wasn't inside, then I climbed back out and ran straight for the pond in the woods, as if he might still be there, waiting for me. It's where he always said he'd set sail from, where *we* would set sail from: he said I could go with him.

The pond in the woods seemed smaller filled with his body. His eyes were open, staring toward the sun, his hands at odd angles, making him look more helpless than resolutely gone. I waded into the water, not saying it, just mouthing the word over and over—*Daddy, Daddy, Daddy, Daddy*—and the water made my jeans and nightgown heavy, filled up my tennis shoes, sucking me down, but I kept on, slogging toward him, the slight movement of his body made by my waves giving me hope.

When I got to him I didn't know what to do. I reached out my hand but I was afraid to touch him. Carefully, I put my hands on both sides of his face, as if to make him listen or to soothe him. I stayed like that for some time, with my hands on his cheeks, memorizing his eyes, the way his face looked—no expression I could recognize or had ever seen, imagining what he would say to me if he could speak. I started to cry and bit my lips to make it stop. *Sissygirl.*

I got out of the water, took off my clothes. It was late December, a day of tulle fog and cold for the valley, but I wanted to be cold, I wanted my skin to go so numb I would stop feeling anything, but it wouldn't stop, even after I took off everything I had on. *Sissygirl.* I bit my own knuckles, drew blood, cried out, bit harder still. Then I ran toward the barbed wire fence, skinnied through the two bottom wires, the barbs cold and sharp grazing my skin. I ran back toward the barn, to see . . . I don't know what I hoped for but maybe this: that he had left some message, if not in the notebook, then there.

Then I remembered the notebook and looked all around me. I must have dropped it. The notebook wasn't there. I bent down my neck, as if humbled or struck, imagined it lying at the bottom of the pond. I ran back to the fence, my heart pounding harder now, hoping I was wrong, climbed through, tearing the skin on my right arm, seeing the blood but not feeling it, ran toward the pond, breathing hard, my chest an ache, feeling the sweat turn cold where the cool air hit it, ran all the way back to the pond, looked around, my eyes blurred with fear and desire. At the edge of the water. On the little pier. Where I'd taken my clothes off. I ran down to the end of the pier, the planks unsteady, shaking beneath me, the pier swaying on its shallow supports. The notebook wasn't there. I stood at the end of the pier for a long time, trying to think what to do, of some other place I could look, something I hadn't yet thought of that might still be possible. I ran all the way around the pond, but I knew it wasn't there, that I hadn't even been on the other side, that it was where I had imagined it: in the water with my father.

I walked out again to the end of the pier, slowly now, flung myself down on my belly, hung my face and arms over the edge, my fingertips touching the water. Only then did I cry, frightening sounds that made me think I was no longer human but some kind of animal.

In this way my mother found me and carried me home, never crying herself, never mentioning our father, only saying, after the funeral, *I'll never be the same,* and she was right, she wasn't; she kept her promise.

I lie down. I lie down on top of the sleeping bag in the triangular bunk at the fore of the boat, close my eyes. I imagine that I am my drowned father, and I try to understand why I did it, what the prologue was, what series of shocks, of what voltage, rendered it possible.

The first year he was gone I made up stories.

He was kidnapped by the Mafia and someone who looked exactly like him was put in his place, murdered, but made to look like a man taking his own life. I'd seen a movie on television about a woman who was raped, who afterward saw her attacker in the street and had him arrested. It was a case of mistaken identity, but the man was saved only moments from the electric chair. After that I kept imagining that I saw my father—out across the field, a dark figure on the road at night, in the grocery store, turning the next corner, always just beyond clear view. The next fall when my mother and I were in town shopping for school clothes, I saw a man who looked almost like my father from the back, the dark hair, longer now, it could have been him these many months later, his hair grown past his collar. My heart began to beat in my chest as if it had a heart of its own. I took my mother's hand and walked faster, nearly dragging her. "Jesse," she said, "Jesse, what's the matter with you?" We caught up to him at the corner, as he waited for the light to turn green so he could cross the street. I looked up at the man's face. It was nothing like my father's. The nose was bigger, his skin mottled, his eyes not deep blue but ordinary brown. I spat at him. And my mother slapped me, ashamed, not knowing why I had done such a thing. The man looked at me, with kindness, I thought, and said, "It's all right, ma'am," as if he knew better than my mother that people had their reasons.

Another story was that it was him all right, dead in the pond in the woods, but he'd been murdered. How else do you explain that he was building a wind machine—*building* something; nobody *builds* something if they know they're going to be dead the next day. And why had he been working on the boat? Explain that, if you can. Nobody sands the deck of a sailboat that's never going to get out of the barn. Murdered. The conclusion was obvious.

There was a television show popular at the time, called "I Led Three Lives," about a double agent who also had a wife and children. I dreamed he was my father and when the spies and counterspies finally caught up with him they buried him in the pond as we had found him. I imagined a moving ceremony in which President Kennedy gave my mother a folded flag, in spite of the fact that my father was a spy. Maybe

I didn't know then what treason was, or maybe I thought my father exempt from the laws of crime and punishment.

When President Kennedy was assassinated, I took this as evidence that my latest hypothesis was correct. He was on my father's side—the ceremony was proof—and so he had to die too.

Another year I thought that it must have been the accident my father had in his last race—that was the reason he killed himself. His silver-blue hardtop had gone through the wall and he'd ended up with splinters in his eardrum, blinding headaches that made him spend days in their bedroom with the shades drawn, a washcloth folded on his forehead, and changed him into someone none of us knew. He would fly into a rage at the slightest noise, and his eyes had gone dead, like there was no one behind them. The headaches finally stopped, but the accident had made him afraid, had destroyed his confidence and his equilibrium, the two things crucial to success as a stock-car racer. He'd been great, had won more races before he was twenty-five than any other driver on the West Coast. Maybe you could be mediocre if you'd never been great, but you couldn't come down to it.

I smooth the cold slippery material of the sleeping bag with my hands. I wonder who put it here. It's nearly new, only slightly damp. Someone has been down here. Who?

My mother.

I get up and look for other evidence. Most of the surfaces are dusty, but there is a second storm lantern that's been brought in from somewhere else—there's no rust on it. I open a new box of Diamond matches next to it, strike a match, and watch the eerie world come to light.

The logbook is still in the shallow shelf above the fold-down table, next to the bottle of J&B. I take it out, open it up to the day of my birthday.

December 17, 1962. More fog, no change in temperature. This is the hour of lead— Remembered, if outlived.

I turn one page, then another, and another, until I come to the page I want.

December 25, 1962.

The date is printed in black ink, in my father's hand, as I remember it. But there is another line below it in blue ink, neatly written in italic script: *I love you. I'm sorry.* These words were not written by my father. These words were not there when I was ten. I would have remembered them; they would have saved such grief, thinking it was me he meant.

My mother must have written them. I trace the words with my finger. See? I hear her say. Your father loved us. He was just too sad to live. Nobody knows why. Maybe if you spend a lifetime thinking about it you will figure it out. Or maybe you will only have a spent lifetime to show for it.

Or it might have been meant not as a message *from* him but as a message to him: *I love you. I'm sorry.* Which was it? And how could one tell?

I try to imagine my mother, here, the logbook in her hands, the pen with blue ink poised above the page. As the dying are supposed to recollect their lives, her life with him appears before me, his gestures, his face, I can see them all clearly. Perhaps she calls out his name for comfort. Both the cause and the cure, how can it be? That tenderness, brutal now knowing the cost. *Dead. Gone.* Why is that so difficult to understand? Because love is mixed up in every evil thing? She starts to cry. The son of a bitch didn't even leave a note. Silence more cruel than any accusation could be. What a strong desire to die it must have taken to drown himself, the body craving air, struggling toward the light, the lungs bursting, and still the mind's simple refusal. Why didn't he just pack up and go instead of taking his own life? As if he couldn't get far enough away.

But out of the corner of my eye, I see it: there I am, the aggrieved child, looking on. Every imagining has me in it. I am not my mother and cannot become her.

I take out the map, spread it out on the wooden table. He had drawn arrows to all of the places we would sail to. Pago Pago. Australia. Alaska. The coast of Ireland. Baja. Marseilles, Monte Carlo, Nice. The Dead Sea.

He said he would take me with him, because I was the only one in the family who could get dressed in under sixty seconds. "We're going to get so far away nobody will ever find us." Who was he trying to get away from? Three kids, always demanding something? "Gimme, buy me, take me," he'd say, mimicking us kids. Or maybe he wanted to get away from my mother, her sceptical gaze. "The old fish-eye," he called it. Or himself. Maybe that was it. I remember a travel book I bought when I was planning to go to Baja three years ago. On the front cover there was a sign that read, WHEREVER YOU GO, THERE YOU ARE. Could the truth be so simple? Or was that reason to suspect it?

It would be a relief to stop asking these questions. Maybe that's why he did it—to stop the noise inside his head. Certainty. Love and suicide are as close as you can get, but suicide is better: you never have to wonder whether you got it wrong.

I go back to the bunk and lie down. Breathe evenly, keep calm. Something will come to you. But what comes is sleep, the old dream.

In the dream I dream of my father. The same dream I've had all my life. It's a common dream, I suppose. There is a mathematical problem I must solve; my father's life depends on it. How do I know that? The dream doesn't say, but I know, the way you know when someone is lying. If I can't solve this problem my father will die.

I work at a large oak desk, with a stack of white bond that never runs out, no matter how many sheets of paper I wad up. The ink of the black marking pen comes off on my hands, numbers tremble on the page, I work feverishly all night long, the unknown deadline coming closer.

As I grew up, the mathematical problem became more complex. Algebra, trigonometry, calculus. In college it was Fermat's last theorem.

Tonight I dreamed the answer. It was simple, obvious. The proof had only three steps. The dream was so vivid that I woke up shaking, my breasts cold with sweat. I stumbled out of the bunk, untangled myself from the sleeping bag, got a pen from the drawer in the galley, the notebook, and wrote it down in the dark.

Then I went back to bed, fell asleep, and dreamed of the boardwalk at Santa Cruz, a place our family used to go in the summers when

I was a child. My father bought me a chocolate-covered frozen banana from the stand by the Giant Dipper. We rode in the first car, our arms above our heads, to show we weren't afraid. He gave me a sapphire blue ring with an expandable gold band that he had won by knocking over three milk cans with a baseball. We had our picture taken in one of those booths with a curtain for a door. The picture came out through the slot outside, like a receipt at the midnight teller's. Proof that my solution was correct.

When I wake up I can't think of the solution. Then I remember the notebook, writing it down. I sit up in the bunk and bump my head on the low ceiling, curse. I look for it under the sleeping bag, then go into the galley, bang my head again, this time on a cupboard, curse louder, pulling out all the drawers, dumping them upside down. No notebook. I go back to the bunk and lie down, try to mentally retrace my steps from the night before. Then I start to laugh. I laugh until I am hoarse, defeated, calm.

I dreamed I was awake.

I sit up in the bunk and bang my head again on the low ceiling, start to curse again in frustration, "Goddamn son of a bitch!" and hear my father's voice: "Goddamn *son* of a bitch, why can't you act like a human being?" He used to say this whenever one of his children had disappointed him, and I always thought he was saying "human bean." Is this the great truth I came back to discover? This random fact?

I can see daylight coming in from above, through the bubble-shaped window in the deck, through the barn's trapdoor. It must be five or six in the morning. Twilight. I smooth out the sleeping bag, zip it closed, roll it up, stuff it in the cubbyhole across from the bunk.

I go into the belly of the boat, careful to keep my head low, sit down on the bench, tie my tennis shoes, simple actions I am surprised to see I can still perform. I feel weak, pure, very light, the way you feel after being badly hurt. The map is open on the table; I fold it up without looking at it, put it back where I found it, close the logbook, and set it in the rack next to the map. I write my father's name in the dust on the table with my forefinger. *Alex Walker. In memoriam.* I make a fist and, in the same motion, rub my forearm through it. I blow out the flame of the storm lamp before I go up the steps, pull the hatch cover back into place behind me.

It's odd to be standing on the deck of a sailboat inside a barn, as if the boat had been stillborn, or as if the builder had no conception of what a sailboat was for. For the first time in my life I wonder how my father proposed to get the boat out of the barn when the time came, without breaking the mast. Or maybe he didn't. Maybe he only said these things to trick himself into living. Maybe he didn't believe his own stories.

I jump down into the mud and straw on the floor of the barn, slipping first one way, then the other, doing a strange dance, righting myself. I walk out the double doors, opening them wide. The barn shudders as the doors bang against the outside wall, and I step out into the uncertain light.

I used to think that that's what death would be like—like the dream: the answer to every question you'd ever asked—simple, obvious—the world coming true in the closing circuits of your brain. I no longer believe it. It will be like this. When I was ten years old I took some pictures of my father the week before he died. When the pictures are developed, there is nothing on them. Every shot is black.

What Light There Is

There are seven of us here—three women, four men—in a boathouse at the end of the pier. We smile shyly and try to avoid one another's eyes. A sign on the wall reads NO FISHING OR SWIMMING IN THE HARBOR.

At exactly ten o'clock one of the women stands up and says, "My name is Sharon St. James." She has the abrupt smile, the quick movements, and the bright eyes of a first-grade schoolteacher. "If you came prepared, you have your toolbox"—she holds hers up—"and your book: *From a Bare Hull* by Ferenc Maté." She opens it up, begins to read.

It has been a long dream. I was thirteen when we used to gather in the basement of a friend to play billiards on a wobbly-legged table the size of an honest suitcase, with tiny clay balls so lumped and pitted that our games seemed more like exercises of faith and hope than displays of skill or concentration. The basement was home to a huge tin furnace that ate sawdust and wood and coal and thumb-wrinkled magazines. From one of these magazines someone had torn a picture, a brown picture of a sailboat, a schooner, I think, and nailed it to the rough inside of the cedar

199

siding. I don't know who put it there, it may have been me; but from that picture on I decided I was going to get that sailboat and sail around the world for the rest of my life.

For most of the years since, I made no conscious effort towards this end. But somehow I had always been certain that sometime, probably any day now, I'd be stepping aboard my boat. . . . The fact that I had absolutely no money, not even enough to accumulate a single noteworthy debt, appeared to have very little bearing on the certainty of my future plans. On the other hand, I knew nothing about sailing boats or their costs, so I was never threatened by the magnitude of the financial chasm between my brown paper schooner and me. . . .

I listen intently, more to the sound of her voice than to the words. A tone of reverence.

She closes the book. "When you finish this course," she says, "you will be able to build your own boat and sail to exotic ports. It can be done. I did it."

A man in army fatigues and a punk haircut raises his hand. "How much will it cost?"

"That depends on the boat and what you start with." She gestures toward the sailboat with a starboard list at the end of the pier, just visible through the window of the boathouse. "That's a Westsail 32," she says, "and I built it from a bare hull, like the book says. It cost me a year of my life and three thousand dollars. That's a conservative estimate. Then I ran it aground in Half Moon Bay. That's why I'm here instead of in Hawaii."

Everyone laughs.

"When it happens to you, you won't think it's so funny," she says. "Now. Open your toolbox and take out your dovetail saw."

We do as she says. The philosopher asks, Why build? The builder asks, Which tools?

"Today we are going to learn to make a straight cut in warped wood. It's difficult *not* to make a straight cut with a dovetail saw, but some of my students have accomplished it."

Again there is laughter, more nervousness than pleasure.

"Are you ready?"

The blade of the saw catches the light, and the weight of the smooth wooden handle is somehow comforting.

"Yes." A chorus.

"Good. Let's get started."

My life has formed a pattern now. I tend bar at a place called the Animal Shelter in a town just south of San Francisco. I've been here for six months, since I left Dubuque, and I've made friends with some of the regulars. They tell me their problems, these eloquently inarticulate men, and I listen, give them stories I've heard somewhere or made up, and when I have no answer, just smile or nod.

I like this job, like the laziness of the afternoons when there are only two or three customers in the bar, the way the sun shines on the dark polished tables, turning them to ebony, the play of lights on the water, the shore lined with fishermen down near Pedro Point. And I like the country music coming from the jukebox, the backslapping and the deep laughter of big men when the bar fills up in the evening. Then again, after closing, I like to sit in the utter silence, the last customer gone, with only the light from the jukebox. I sit at the table in the far corner with my feet up, smoking a cigarette, and watch the amber liquid in cut-glass decanters catch the light, admire the newly washed glasses shining in the mirror above the long oak bar. Some nights Monte comes in around closing time, and we'll share a late breakfast at the café across the street.

Every weekday morning, with the exception of Tuesday, I come here and write in a notebook that I have been keeping, on and off, since I was ten. The bar looks different now, before the wooden shades are drawn, the slats letting in just enough light to turn the bottles of Jim Beam and Bacardi into icons, the long expanse of warm oak into an altar, the trestle tables and benches into places of prayer. On Tuesday mornings I take boat-building lessons down at the marina.

Every Saturday morning at two A.M., when the bar closes, I make the two-hour trip to my mother's house, where I work with my hands—the only real talent I have—and with plane and hammer and saw and caulking, rebuilding the boat my father began, planning the trip he spoke of taking. I come out of the drafty barn only for food or sleep, the rare conversation with my mother. On Sunday nights I come back here, a little one-room beach shack with a view of Pedro Point to the south, the Marin headlands to the north.

These are the minor events that make up my life, a sort of circular movement, like that made with a pen attached to a gyro, something I saw at the Exploratorium last week on a trip into the city with Sheila. Each circle so close to the last that there is no discernible difference between any two, though if you watch long enough the series of circles rises or falls, moves to the left or the right, depending on how the gyro is set, the angle of the pen, and the position of the viewer.

But at every moment during each week with its invisible move-ment, the thing that does not change is this waiting. There is no way of knowing if the address Lucky gave Kathleen when he left Dubuque is still good, though there is some reason to doubt it, since he told her then that after seeing some old friends in New York, he thought he might move on to Alaska. There is no way of knowing, too, if his mail will be forwarded, if he will get my letter, and if he does, what he will make of it, whether the words I have put down here will be sufficient.

I sometimes think it's odd that Kathleen should be our only possible link, that my finding him again depends on his loyalty to her—a person of little consequence, I thought, one I took no time to understand. It's something to consider. When I call her from my mother's house, on Sunday nights, before heading back, Kathleen is kind but not encouraging. She told me that she and Lucky were lovers briefly, years ago, but except for the occasional drink, "That's as far as it went." Her words. So there's little hope he will write or call, unless one day he is seized with an inexplicable longing for a time he may regret. I don't know.

What I do know is this: the major movements of our lives are made under conditions of ignorance and uncertainty as to the patterns they will eventually form. We can misconceive our own desires and their objects, believing that because two things are alike they are of equal value. It matters not only what properties they share but how they came to be as they are. As there could not be two identical spirals differing only in their points of origin. Some relations are particular. When I tried to explain this to Monte one night after closing, he said he thought he understood.

I know my mother does, and in that knowledge we have become allies, if not in all things. She isn't what you would call a forthcoming person, but now and then when I am home for the weekend, she will tell me a story about my father, something that happened before I was born. How, for example, one Sunday afternoon he brought home a trunk full of old pictures, the half-charred remains of someone's estate he had found at the dump. He spent hours looking through them, she said, then carefully cut glass and made oak frames for those of the photographs that were undamaged or could be restored. He hung them in the hallway. When she asked him why on earth he would want to save pictures of strangers, he said, "That's a man's *life* there. Someone should save them." It doesn't sound like him, like something he would do, a misanthrope who didn't like his picture taken. The story doesn't explain anything but still I like to imagine him doing it. Someone should.

I close the notebook and put it in a drawer beneath the cash register. I put on my apron, get the ice bucket, go into the back room, fill it, and carry it up to the front, dump it in the ice bin—it takes four trips—then I put my mixers in the corners, cut up oranges, lemons, limes, run hot soapy water in one sink, run another sink for rinsing, and then wipe down the bar, set out clean ashtrays.

Jack Mosley comes in right at one, and I pour him a shot of J&B before punching up some songs on the jukebox. He always talks about the same thing: his son, John Benjamin Mosley, "the third," who was killed in a car accident.

"He was a wiry little kid and didn't grow up much bigger. About your size." He draws the height with his hand at his neck. "But he was all-state quarterback in '68. Faster than a jackrabbit, slipperier than a catfish." This is the place where he grins, then his face goes dark, like those sudden storms they get off the coast up farther north. "He wanted to be a lawyer, you know." I nod. "Not to make money, you understand. But to help people without it get justice." I nod again. "A fine boy," he says, and I agree, trying to reconstruct his son's features from this brief history. "Close to your age, he would've been."

I smile, thinking that a thing like being the same age might have made me and the dead son of a fisherman classmates; in this small town, friends.

"The day it happened I was up north, getting the trawler engine rebuilt, and I didn't hear about it until I got back late that night. That always made me feel bad, that I wasn't there. I know it's stupid but I think maybe I could have done something. You know?" He stares at his hands, turns them over, as if he might find some detail he's missed, something that would have made the difference.

"The CHP said the truck hit him head-on doing seventy, eighty. He didn't stand a chance. The drunk son of a bitch just came *clear* across that white line, right there by Devil's Slide where there's nowhere to go but down. The drunk son of a *bitch*!" He wipes a hand over his face, but his expression doesn't change. "They called the ambulance and rushed him to the hospital, but it was too late. The gearshift pierced him through the heart. Can you believe that?"

I nod but try not to imagine this part too vividly.

"The head of the thing'd come off a long time ago—it was just a piece of plastic, you know—and nobody'd ever bothered to screw it back on." He shakes his head. "Never even made it to Emergency." He's quiet a moment and I wonder what scene he's reconstructing.

The ending is always the same. "It's a shame," he says finally. "A crying shame."

I pour him another shot of J&B, on the house, and turn up the jukebox. Jim Reeves is singing "Welcome to My World."

Arthur comes in and I set him up at the other end of the bar with a rum and Coke. "Here you go," I say, and he smiles. He's about eighty, I think, and he's not with it most of the time, but he's a gentle drunk, and once in a while you can get a glimpse of what he must have been like: a good belly laugher, a thoughtful man. He said to me once, when I asked him what he wanted, "I want the kind of love that takes a long time. But I'll settle for a rum and Coke."

The afternoon slides into evening—washing glasses and setting up drinks, making small talk with the people, mostly men, who come in, and watching the moving waves through the bright rectangular panes of the oak-framed windows. It was a slower afternoon than usual, and tonight is quiet for a Friday night. Only Ron Silva and Jeff Reilly playing liars' dice, Jack Mosley, still at the other end of the bar drinking J&B, old Arthur, talking to himself as usual, and a couple I don't know in the corner.

To pass the time, I cut up more oranges, lemons, limes, though almost everyone in the place drinks beer or ungarnished well drinks.

I polish the bar with the dishtowel and pour Arthur another drink. He's laughing to himself now, his hands gesticulating comically, like a traffic cop on speed.

The woman of the couple in the corner comes over and puts a quarter in the jukebox. I look at her—short dark hair, brown eyes that say too much, give away nothing, a nondescript pair of jeans and a long-sleeved black blouse—trying to guess what she will play. Linda Ronstadt, maybe. She looks back at me, squirming in her pigeonhole, I think, and plays Willie Nelson.

It's not supposed to be that way . . .

I study the Lone Tree beer sign above the mirror, the unsettling effect of the moving water, the harsh blue light. I look at old Arthur, who has raised his voice in response to the music, his head cocked to one side, then the other, as if playing both parts in a conversation. I wonder what he is saying, whether his musings are of remembered happiness or repetitions of humiliating scenes.

When the song is over, the woman of the couple in the corner gets up and walks out of the bar, leaving the heavy curtains slightly parted so that a sliver of light from outside falls across the face of the bewildered man, cutting it in half, diagonally, half light, half dark. He sits there for a while, looking around, as if someone might give him directions, tell him what to do next. Then he gets up from the table, comes over, and sits down at the bar.

I pop the top off another Lone Tree, set it in front of him, thinking he and I went to different schools together.

"Thanks," he says, raising his beer bottle.

"How's it going?"

"Not good," he says, looking back at the open curtain. Up close I can see he's much younger than I thought. Twenty-two, twenty-three. A kid.

"Think she'll come back?" I ask, none of my business.

He half laughs, shakes his head, stares into the mouth of his beer bottle, then tilts it up. "I don't know," he says, before taking a sip.

I stand and watch the rain falling through the dark glass, the ocean black beyond it, except for the white of the slow-breaking waves.

It's been a long night. The clock over the bar reads 1:45.

"Last call," I say, thinking of the two-hour drive to my mother's house, the boat in the barn, waiting.

Jack Mosley is the only taker. "One for the road," he says, holding up his empty glass. It looks, in this light, like a fist raised in protest.

After thirteen hours of straight shots, he must be in pretty bad shape. But he lives over at the trailer park, just a short walk from here.

I take away his wadded-up napkin, lay down another, pour him a shot of J&B in a clean glass.

" 'Sa shame," he says drunkenly. I put my hand on his, light on dark from days fishing. "He was a wiry little kid, you know, and didn't grow up much bigger. 'Bout your age, he would've—"

"Tomorrow's my birthday," I tell him, because I don't want to hear the same story again. "I'll be thirty-five. Middle-aged. Hard to believe, huh? I'm too young to be that old."

"Old enough to know better," he says, "but too young to resist. Just the right age." He winks, raises his glass.

"Thanks," I say, picking up the six quarters he's left me and dropping them into the tip jar. They make a sound like harsh bells ringing.

"What are you going to do to celebrate?"

"I haven't decided."

"Well, you should do something. You're thirty-five only once, you know."

"That's true," I say.

He holds up his glass again. "Celebrate, goddamn it! *Some-*thing." For a moment he is not himself, mourner at his own life.

"I will," I promise.

"You better. You're dead a long time." He laughs.

"To tell you the truth, I've been thinking about moving on."

"Where to?"

"Alaska."

His eyes brighten in the light of the Lone Tree beer sign.

"When business is this slow—you know, when all I've got for company most of the night is old thoughts and older songs on a jukebox, I long . . . for more dramatic landscapes. A fire in the forest. The ancient ice of glaciers," I say grandly.

"Land of the Midnight Sun," he says, in the same grand tone of voice. "The Last Frontier." He pauses a slow moment, dreaming the dream of drunk men; of all of us. "I've never been to Alaska," he says. "In fact, I've never been off the peninsula."

"You should go," I tell him. "Take a trip. What's stopping you?"

He raises his glass. "It's a full-time job," he says, "but somebody's got to do it."

I laugh, shake my head.

At five minutes to two I turn the dimmer switch to the right and start cleaning up.

My mother holds up the dark blue wool coat, one sleeve slightly longer than the other. "What do you think?"

"You actually finished it."

"Did you doubt your old mother?"

"Yes. I confess I did."

"A person can change," she says in a haughty voice, raising her chin, lowering her eyelids to half mast.

She puts it on and does a pirouette in front of the full-length mirror on her bedroom door. "Your father always liked this color." She looks at me in the mirror. "What a shame," she says, "that he couldn't live to see you kids all grown up—his oldest daughter a teacher, his son a policeman, and his youngest child a world-class dilettante."

"I prefer to think of myself as well rounded."

"A failure to be serious," she says. Then she takes the coat off and holds it up by the collar for me to put on. "For your birthday."

"Thank you." I am surprised and moved, more by the fact that she hates sewing than by anything else. "What are *you* going to be when you grow up?" I ask.

"Old," she says and laughs. "I think I'll make a good old woman, don't you? Sitting out on that porch in the rocking chair, shaking my cane at the squirrels and the toads."

Yes. She will make a good old woman. "Do you think you'll ever get married again?"

"I did that once," she says. "What about you?"

"Oh, I don't know." My voice drifts off and she doesn't push. I think of something Lucky said once: If you want a guarantee, buy a refrigerator.

"There's a man," she says. "But it's not the same as with your father."

"I know what you mean."

"I remember the night we met."

I smile as if my life depends on it and she continues.

"It was at a ballroom dance at the Cocoanut Grove."

"Santa Cruz," I say, picturing the dance hall, three stages, remembering the first time a boy asked me to dance, the summer I was twelve.

"Yes. He stood at the side of the room watching me, I thought, but it's hard to tell in the dark. You can think someone is gazing in admiration when they're really only drunk, focusing on a spot on the far wall to keep from falling down."

I laugh.

She pulls her long hair back with one hand, cocks a shoulder, the other hand on her hip, fingers back, and gives me a sultry stare. "But I was watching him. I was saying a lot on that floor."

I let out a long slow whistle and she smiles.

"Well, after about an hour, he came up and invited me not to dance."

"*Not* to dance?"

"Yes. What did you have in mind? I asked, so innocent. His hands did all the talking, gesturing at the door, the night." She looks toward the window as if she could see it all over again. "A proper young woman who is slightly drunk might let him take her hand, follow him out. I did," she says. "I followed him to a red Jaguar with the top down. We had to sell it when Ellen was born. Not exactly a family car, you know."

I think of Lucky's car and wonder what became of it, if he ever got it back. "What happened then?"

"I remember exactly what he said. He said, You have nice legs, lady. I got in."

"My mother the siren."

"I don't remember what we talked about. But the words weren't the point."

"I can see that."

"He drove me home. I remember there was a full moon. When we were in my parents' driveway he shut off the lights, put up the top. You could get moonburn, he said."

I laugh. Once she was naive. Silly even.

"I said I'd take my chances. Then it's already too late, he said. That's one of the symptoms." She smiles. "He looked at me mournfully, shook his head. There's only one way to cure moonburn, he said. Then he demonstrated." She smiles again, as if at an old snapshot I could never be in. "It was the best kiss I've ever had."

The familiar pain begins at the back of my neck then spreads, through my arms, my legs, but this time I don't try to stop it, I let it come, wave after wave of it, until it is an effort to remain, as against a stiff wind one struggles to go forward, a person and not merely a subject of pain. "Why?"

She turns her head away, raises her hand in a gesture I cannot interpret. "I blamed myself," she says. "A man can't stand to always be looked at with a fish-eye. Bringing down his dreams, he called it. He said I was always bringing down his dreams. Is that true? Was I?"

"I blamed myself, too," I say. "I thought I stole his soul. By taking those pictures."

"Even now I think of it—was there something I could have said?" She looks at me hard. "Was there?"

In the seventh picture he rises from the water, soul intact, his hand touching her hair, leaning toward the woman she would become, whispering words the camera cannot hear.

"I don't know."

She turns away, walks over to the window, pulls the curtain back, looks out. For all the light knows it could be dawn instead of dusk, the distant tree a human figure moving toward us.

"There is no known cure for moonburn," she says.

I think of Lucky and go to stand beside her. "No." From where I am I can see what she sees, I can hear him breathing, I can feel our hearts beating as we stand there holding each other, just holding each other. Like this.

The pond in the woods looks different at night. I wonder why—why should the simple lack of light so change it, the darkness alter its depth, move its outlying edges farther back into the trees? I walk down to the end of the pier, lie flat on my belly, hang my head over the edge, let my arms dangle down. The waterline comes up to the knob of each wrist, and I think, That's all I've grown in twenty-five years, less than the length of a human hand, not much.

I get up on my knees, feel something piercing, pull out a splinter, lick my index finger, and press it to the small wound. Then I stand all the way up, dust the bits of wood from the pier off my breasts, my thighs. I walk back to the other end of the pier, cross the salt-grass hills in the dark, feel the air warm around my body, not cold at all, winter spring.

I open the double doors of the barn, hear a creak, then a groaning sound. The moon is a quarter moon and doesn't cast much light. I find the rope ladder, climb up to the deck. Soon my eyes adjust to the dark and I can see the hatch. I open it up, back down into the boat, careful to keep my head low, find my way with my hands to the table in the galley, pick up the storm lamp and the box of matches, light the lamp, carry it back up the stairs. The teak deck, just refinished, glows in the yellow light. The hull of the boat is patched, and the name changed, block letters painted in black. The brand-new sails are neatly folded at the fore of the boat, waiting to be rigged. I set the storm lamp on the deck and climb down the rope ladder.

The floor of the barn is covered with hay and mud, from the rain coming through the barn's trapdoor. I begin to clear the hay away, then I see the pitchfork leaning against the wall of the barn; it glistens in the light of the lamp and I get it to make the job easier, remembering the time my brother heaved it at me like a javelin, in one of the many barn wars we had with bales of hay for forts, and one prong stuck in my thigh. It was a dangerous game we played. I pile the loose hay in a circle, about ten feet back. When I have cleared the ground, I get the shovel from just inside the barn door and begin to dig a shallow ditch around the boat, moving the storm lamp as I go.

When the ditch is dug, I run a hose from the spigot outside the barn to the ditch and fill it up. Then I pour gasoline on the circle of hay around the boat, set it on fire, feel the thrill of power at the first easy blaze, watch it rise higher, soon reaching the walls of the barn. The fire starts to make my face hot, though I am standing near the boat, so I climb the rope ladder up to the deck. And in this way I can better see the path of the blaze, which wall is likely to go first. There is no breeze at all tonight, so each wall will fall of its own accord, depending upon how it was built. Freud says that the mind under stress is like a crystal thrown to the floor: it doesn't break into haphazard pieces but comes apart along its lines of cleavage into fragments whose boundaries, though invisible, were predetermined by the crystal's structure. That's how I think of the barn, and I am betting that the walls will fall away instead of falling in, and that the roof will fall clear of the boat or that the damage will be minimal. It's dangerous, I know, very risky, but I have tried and cannot imagine another way to do it.

The fire has reached the north wall, and even in the dark I can see the black traveling up toward the roof; then the second wall blazes, and the third, and finally the last wall is burning. I have not imagined this part well enough. I didn't know that the heat would be so stifling or that the smoke and floating debris would make it this hard to breathe.

I go down into the boat to get a cloth to soak with water from the hose to cover my face. Inside the boat the blaze outside is altered, as if seen from inside a glass ball, one of those paperweight worlds I had wanted as a child, filled now with fire instead of snow, a man-made hell. I take a cloth from under the sink in the galley, then climb back up the steps. I jump down onto the ground, where the mouth of the hose is running water, and wet the rag, put it over my face, then climb back up to the deck. My eyes are starting to burn. It's getting hotter and hotter. Even with the wet cloth covering my mouth it's getting hard to breathe. I am afraid, and I imagine being overcome by the fire before any wall falls, and my mother finding the body like this, the charred remains, in the morning, and what she will think. I start to weep, mourner at my own death, then an alien thought comes to me: I want to live. The roof is burning now, at the edge of the north and east walls, then the next corner starts. I hadn't guessed it would happen this way but the roof caves in first, making a sweep from northeast to south, and parts of it hit the mast but fall free. Then the north wall comes down. But instead of falling in or out, it buckles halfway, folds in upon itself, like the face of a cut flower closing. I laugh out loud, as if I had foreseen the exact manner of its destruction, as if I had planned it all. Then the next wall goes, creating a wind that fans the fire and blows debris onto the deck of the boat. I try to kick the burning debris from the deck, without success, and finally give up and use my hands to throw it off, burning them badly I get down on my knees, wrap my hands in the wet cloth that has fallen at my feet. Then I hear a sound—like the sound of a firecracker or the crack of a gun—and I see the last two walls cave in, toward the southwest corner of the barn, leaving only the frame still standing. There is more light around the boat now, and the air is easier to breathe.

The last time I felt like this we had just come into Juneau, my husband and I, on the ferry from Seattle. It was four in the morning when the *Malaguena* pulled into dock, and my husband woke me up, helped me on with my new coat, the alien scarf and gloves: we were coming from Arizona. I was only half awake when we stepped down from the ramp onto the pier, looked around us. The whole side of the mountain was on fire. Everyone stood—there were thirty or forty of us beside the dark water—stood staring up at it, our faces lit by the blaze. "This moment is holy," my husband said, and whatever harm I had caused or suffered I forgot.

Now I see the finished boat, all teak and bright sway of sail and rope, pulling out of the bay. I can hear my mother already. "A dilettante," she will say, when I tell her I'm leaving. "A failure to be serious." And maybe she is right. There are nights that I agree, see the danger, share her fear: What happens next? How will it end? What will some future self make of me?

But on the clearest days, like tomorrow will be—when the sky is the blue of a child's coloring book and the light has returned to the water its rightful magic—I will stand at this altar and think of the pond in the woods that led to the sea, my father's laughter. I am very serious, I will tell her then. A dreamer of some distinction. I am becoming the world.

The foregoing synopsis conveys an approximate notion of my novel. It was extremely long. In finished form the typescript filled three separately bound volumes, each of roughly four to five hundred typed pages. Like every beginning writer, I longed for publication. In my thoughtless audacity I turned once again to Thomas Mann, with whom I had maintained a sporadic correspondence, asking him to recommend my book to his publisher. He did so. It was rejected. The great man, who had never set eyes on me, winner of the Nobel Prize, author of masterworks like *Death in Venice* and *The Magic Mountain*, sent me a kindly letter.

> *Dear Mr. Lord:*
>
> *With you I am disappointed about the failure at Knopf's. He had written me that your person made a very favorable impression on him. But even if his office's verdict of your novel was negative, I feel you should not give up the matter without a struggle. After all, Knopf is not the only publisher to be considered. You should try to offer your work to one or the other house. If in the end your book should be judged too unaccomplished for publication, you will find consolation in renewed creative efforts which will benefit by your growing years and inner maturing.*
>
> > *With kindest wishes*
> > *Very sincerely yours,*
> > *Thomas Mann*

I did not seek another publisher. My manuscript made its way to the wastebasket, and I entrusted my future literary aspirations to the problematic effect of inner maturing. In the fullness of decades this has had to do what it could for the story of my queer war.

So begins Peter's mystical ascent toward the culmination of his purpose. In the person of Hans he is held for questioning about the apparent murder of the American. His answers are studied, tending to be convoluted and lengthy, punctuated by laborious teleological asides. The interrogators weary, patience oftentimes tried beyond forbearance. They have no alternative, however, but to abide and heed. The proceedings eventually lead to a formal charge of murder in the first degree with critical malice aforethought. Hence a court is convened in Frankfurt-am-Main to consider the charge, hear the accused, render a verdict, and deliver a sentence.

The hearing of the accused by the court is prolonged. This proves inevitable because it presently becomes evident that the accused who stands before his judges is none other than the man once known as the Ogre of Ohrdruf. He proves prepared to speak at almost interminable length, determined, moreover, that the court should hearken with tireless discernment, virtually with reverence, to the intricate, sometimes lyrical, but always metaphysical ratiocinations with which he endeavors to calibrate, as it were, the confession of his unspeakable crimes.

Witnesses, to be sure, are not needed, but they cry out to be heard, and are heard by the score, shrieking, weeping, gesticulating at the monster, and demanding divine retribution. Thus the trial endures and endures, an ordeal of endurance for all. For all save the accused, who perseveres with equanimity, surveying the spectacle of his guilt as if the chorus of condemnation and the courtroom itself were but providential elements of his imagination.

When at long last it comes time to hear verdict and sentence, the breath of the chamber is itself almost exhausted. Guilty as charged. Consequently to be hanged by the neck until dead.

It is a day of heavenly radiance that morning when Peter is led to the scaffold. As the noose is fixed about his throat, it may have appeared to the few spectators present that his mouth is touched by something rather like a saintly smile.

Be that as it may, when the trap is sprung, Peter glimpses as he falls a flash of brilliance in which seems to be subsumed the love that moves the sun and the other stars.

•

don and power, unable to hear the screams of a victim above his very own gasps of exertion—again and again—until the climactic instant, whereupon he stumbled away into the mists of eternity. And in a twinkling he had become as one possessed, the demiurge of cruelty, while at the same time each night at its darkest seduced him with remorse and he sobbed at the remoteness of redemption, though the exhaustion of dawn restored the beast to its bloodstained frenzy. So Hans became known as the Ogre of Ohrdruf.

When American forces advanced across the Neisse River and captured Schloss Wartburg, threatening Thuringia, the Ogre of Ohrdruf managed to slip away, tramp north to Erfurt, and there insinuate himself into a straggle of ordinary POWs marching under light guard southwest through the woods toward the Rhineland detention camps, and it was in Mannheim Camp No. 3 that Hans and Peter met.

That was the story told to the ear of darkness in Bad Kreuznach. Atonement is all Hans lives for, the bliss of expiation. Yet he fears other DPs might recognize the erstwhile ogre and do unto him as he has done to so many others. He grasps Peter in his arms, praying for deliverance though he knows he has no right to it. Peter says that it need not be so, something could be, something *should* be, done to make things right. Peter swears that this could come about.

Shortly thereafter one evening Hans asks Peter not to come to the camp the following day. During the night, however, Peter has a troubling premonition as of impending crisis. He hurries to the camp.

In a corner of the lager set apart from the rest he comes upon the naked, bloody corpse of his twin. The body is lacerated with cuts, wrists, ankles, and groin brutally mangled. The jagged end of a broken Coca-Cola bottle lies at hand. But the brow is clear. Peter touches the dead cheek, cold as a stone. His fingertip leaves a dimple. An inexplicable transport, exquisite and dreadful, seizes him. Is this murder by vengeful compatriots? Is this suicide? Death does not engage in repartee.

The dead boy's clothing lies carefully folded beside him, his identification disk on top. Peter does not have to be hurried by the unnatural to undress in an instant, scatter his own uniform round about, hang his dog tags about Hans's throat, take the dead man's disk on its greasy string for his own neck, and pull on the abandoned clothing of the deceased, sidling away in the obscurity of the mutilated remains of an American soldier.

which Hans himself has been, and continues to be, unable or unprepared to clarify. Inasmuch as the German Army has surrendered without condition and in principle no longer exists, the German prisoners kept in detention have no recourse to outside protection and become disarmed enemy persons. Hans, being a DP with the question mark of his past hindering his future, finds himself assigned early in June for transfer to Bad Kreuznach. The parting of the two friends presents itself as unacceptable.

Postings for intelligence agents have become lax. Peter promptly transfers himself to Bad Kreuznach, where he finds Hans in painful condition, mental as well as physical, once more disheveled and filthy, crestfallen, given to periodic seizures of uncontrollable weeping. When pressed to explain, he finally blurts in a whisper the ghastly story of the gap in his past. Inducted at age seventeen into the Waffen SS, he was trained and served for a time as a carter in an artillery maintenance battalion, whereupon an abrupt error of registration allotments transferred him overnight for duty as a guard at a concentration camp in the Thuringian hill country near a town called Ohrdruf.

If absolute evil can be collated, conditions in the camp at Ohrdruf were of the worst. Guards as well as kapos flogged the inmates with metal-studded whips, pissed in their faces, and set maddened dogs to tear off the genitals of naked boys. Hans was stricken down to his entrails again and again by the spectacle of suffering, its clamor and stench, the puling screams, excrement, gasps and grunts, the laughter of the guards, emptied eye sockets of dying children, and agony of the Jewish virtuoso playing *An die Musik* on a battered violin while mutilated girls made love to the boots of an Albanian.

Still, between splayed fingers pressed to his face Hans ogled in spite of himself the orgy of cruelty. Here were the kapos splattered with mucus and blood, grinning as they tortured Russian officers, beckoning with sadistic forefingers to Hans, to incite him, to excite him, to tempt him to participate in the satanic debauch. Beside himself with terror and agitation, even as his bowels heaved, yet tempted by quivering nerve ends in his belly, Hans moved closer and closer to default of the senses, touching the handle of a whip and abruptly swooning into the blackness of overpowering excitement, and he did as the demon in us all decreed he must do: submitted entirely to the deafening aban-

Most of the action of this novel, which never received a title, takes place in a prison camp for captured German soldiers during the last weeks of the European war and for an unspecified period of time thereafter. The protagonist is a young American sergeant named Peter, a military intelligence agent, speaking impeccable German, assigned to work in this camp, his duties unspecified, though with considerable authority. Peter's background, troubled formative years, and troubling wartime experiences are related in order to prefigure a disposition for transcendental experience.

In the lager over which this young man chooses to exercise a certain authority he forms semifriendly relations with the Lagerführer. He then encounters a young prisoner, filthy and disheveled, sullen and withdrawn, but physically sturdy and, beneath the dirt, handsome, with whom he becomes friendly, providing him with cigarettes, soap, and extra food from the PX. This attachment is emotional but never sexual, because in Peter's constitution the sexual element is strangely suspended, allowing, perhaps, for a superior claim on other senses. The prisoner's name is Hans. His background is described in detail, for he lived through the tragic and corrupting experiences pitting his young unworldliness against the Nazi machinery of evil.

A bond is joined between the two young men. They grow aware that they are united—without realizing quite how or why—by an affinity beyond the sphere of ordinary experience. A joint identity, so to speak, of spirit turns out to be well reflected in the physical. When Hans is cleaned up, better fed, and decently clothed, he stands revealed in the flesh as a viable portrait of Peter. The two youths are stunningly, almost supernaturally similar in personal appearance—stature, facial features, color of eyes and hair, the very shape of fingernails—and even in expressive mannerisms to such a degree, for example, that when they laugh, the right eyelids of both flutter slightly so that they appear to be winking at the world. In short, they are much more alike than the most identical of identical twins, a fact recognized with astonishment by the other prisoners but not by Allied personnel, who have no occasion to see them together.

When the European war comes to a conclusion and POWs begin to be released, Hans is further detained. There is something amiss in his record, a period or posting unaccounted for, blank and puzzling,

EPILOGUE

The return to civilian life for soldiers from overseas was widely held to be difficult, not to say traumatic. Hiding in my bedroom, listening to Beethoven's last quartet and rereading *Tonio Kröger*, I made fun of this notion. I slept late, appeared downstairs only for meals, did talk of this and that, returned to my room, lay on my bed, and made friends with stress. Thus passed unbeknownst to me a winter and a spring.

My parents grew concerned, asked what I wanted to do. I replied that I wanted to write a book. I didn't set about doing this immediately, but I did eventually go back into the world of bumblebees, automobiles, and boys, though what I did there other than to think about writing doesn't signify.

By the mercy of its means the book at last began to grow on me. As for its growth, its purpose, theme, meaning, and elaboration and, above all, its egregious pretentiousness, it may seem that some *apologia pro opera sua* would be appropriate, but I have none to offer because the scenario speaks for itself.

To give conceptual substance, as it were, to my book, I planned from the beginning to base it structurally, thematically, and symbolically upon *The Divine Comedy* by Dante, referring metaphorically, indeed, to certain specific passages and even using whenever it seemed figuratively cogent Dante's own phraseology. If this be preposterous, it may be provocative to recall that Joyce's *Ulysses* as well as *The Magic Mountain* played crucial roles in the evolution of my dreams and aspirations.

·